THE FOX, THE DOG, AND THE KING

The Cassie Tam Files, Book Two

Matt Doyle

A NineStar Press Publication

Published by NineStar Press
P.O. Box 91792,
Albuquerque, New Mexico, 87199 USA.
www.ninestarpress.com

The Fox, the Dog, and the King

Printed in the USA
First Edition
July, 2018

Print ISBN: 978-1-949340-15-0

Also available in eBook, ISBN: 978-1-949340-12-9

Warning: This book contains scenes of graphic violence and mention of dogfights.

New Hopeland City may have been built to be the centerpiece of the technological age, but some remnants of the old world still linger. The tools of the trade have changed, but the corruption remains the same, even in the criminal underworld ...

When PI Cassie Tam and her girlfriend Lori try to make up for their recent busy schedules with a night out at the theatre to watch the Tech Shift performer Kitsune, the last thing they expected was for Cassie to get a job offer. But some people are never off the clock, and by the end of the evening, Cassie has been drawn into a mundane but highly paid missing pet case. Unfortunately, in New Hopeland City, even something as simple as little lost dog can lead you down some dark paths.

Until now, Cassie wasn't aware that there even was a rabbit hole, let alone how far down it goes.

Chapter One

"CAZ! BE CAREFUL!" Charlie lets out an exasperated sigh, and adds, "Those are new cushions."

I stop wiping the freshly spilt coffee on my trouser leg with my hand and give her an only partially serious indignant look.

"What? You can handle a bit of caffeine, the material can't."

"Terribly sorry," I reply, relaxing back into Charlie's couch. I raise my mug daintily to my mouth and take a sip, complete with a raised pinkie finger, then place the mug gently back onto the coffee table between us. "Better?"

Charlie almost gags on her own coffee as she tries to stifle a laugh and ends up dribbling some of the molten goodness down her chin.

"Oh, do be careful, Charlotte. These are new cushions," I say, throwing in my best mock posh tone.

And now we both laugh, the sound bringing with it warm memories of times long gone.

The woman opposite me, Charlotte Goldman, is one of the top synth stimulant dealers in the city—an Elite Seller in fact. She's also my ex-girlfriend. We only dated for a year but our breakup, while not what you'd call nasty, shook me and left me far too snarky to be dateable for a long time afterward. Then, Lori Redwood came knocking. She hired me to investigate her brother Eddie's death. He was a VR junkie, and I honestly thought that the case would be simple when I took it. It wasn't. For many reasons.

Somehow, Lori managed to break through my previously impenetrable walls, and one of the positive changes that she's set about making in my life since we started dating is to make sure I reconnected with Charlie. I'm grateful, but I don't think her intentions were entirely pure. Our now mutual friend, Jane, once told me that Lori had a habit of dating assholes. Part of me thinks that having me talk her up to my ex, who, if I'm being honest, I *was* still a little hung up on, is a way of boosting her own confidence in *us*. I could be wrong, of course. It has, unfortunately, been known to happen from time to time.

No matter what Lori's reasons were, I *am* glad she did it. I've missed Charlie. Missed the way she makes me feel when I'm around her. Up until recently, I thought that was entirely due to the romance, but looking at it now, I know that I was wrong. I would be lying if I told myself I could look back on it and say we were *never* suited in that way, but the things I missed the most don't need romance thrown in. Relaxing over a hot drink, catching up on what we've been up to, that sort of thing.

"And what's that smile for?" Charlie asks, smiling wickedly with the question.

"I was just thinking about how much I'm enjoying being able to kick back around someone and be the person who isn't an investigator for hire, stuck in the middle of something potentially nasty."

Charlie lets out a short, gentle laugh and pushes her long auburn hair back behind her ears. "Having trouble opening up around Lori, huh?"

"It takes a while with me. You know that."

"Yeah. I had, what? Three, three and a half months of grumpy Miss Sleuth until you started relaxing properly around me?"

I nod. "Honestly, I've just been so busy since the Locke trial that I haven't had as much time with her as I'd like."

"And yet you're making plenty of time for me," Charlie replies, shaking her head sadly.

"Lori works, too. We talk a lot, but meeting up is the difficult bit. I'm heading straight there from here, though. We're gonna make a night of it. You just happened to be on the way," I add with a cheeky wink.

"Oh, I bet you are." Charlie laughs, ignoring my jibe. "Does she have something picked out for you already? A nice little PVC one-piece, perhaps?"

I sigh and drop my face in my hands. At some point, Charlie realised that she knew a few people who knew Lori. Then she found out that Lori frequented Tourniquet, the late-night cafe where we had our first date. It's a nice place: good food, good drink, good prices, all you could want, really. But, as soon as Charlie discovered that its primary patrons are members of the local fetish scene, her mind went straight to PVC and leather, and she decided that would make great material to crack jokes at my expense. Yes, I *am* glad Lori helped me reconnect with Charlie. At times like this, though, I could kill her for it.

"It's not like that," I whine.

Rather than push ahead with her assault like she has the last couple of times, Charlie goes quiet for a moment. "Caz, were you into stuff like that when you and I dated?"

"No. I never even thought about stuff like *that* when we were together."

"I thought not." She smirks. "You're a relationship chameleon."

I look up, sure that my face is a picture of confusion. "A what?"

"A relationship chameleon. It means that you change when you're dating someone and become more like them. Like how you were into retro rock when we met, and then suddenly took a major interest in jazz when you found out that *I* like it."

"I just never gave jazz a chance before," I groan. "And I still like retro rock. Besides, everyone changes a little when they're in a relationship."

"True." Charlie nods. "We all adapt or pick up little things here and there. I, for one, learned how to comfort a big, scary detective who's a massive wuss when it comes to jump scares. You change a lot, though. Do you remember how you told me about changing your drinking habits when you were dating what's her name...uhm..." Charlie clicks her fingers, trying to remember the name.

"Dani," I fill in the blank. "Dani Cole."

"Dani," Charlie repeats, pointing a finger at me in triumph. "You barely touched alcohol until you met her, but by the time you'd started seeing me you were drinking at least one beer a night. I bet you still do. It's not just habits, though; your personality alters too. You were really shy when we first met, then while you were with me, you started adopting some of my snark. From what you told me about how you were in your youth, I reckon you got the shyness from someone else."

"Or maybe your snark is catching?"

"I prefer so lovable that people can't help but imitate it, but I'll take it. And when we split, you reverted to a mix of moody and shy. It was like you didn't know where to focus yourself anymore. And now you're suddenly a bit more confident and...I dunno, jokey."

"Maybe I was just miserable alone, and now I'm happy again?" I try.

"Or maybe you're adopting some of Lori into yourself. Caz, I can tell when what you're saying is you and when it's something else you're trying to take on. I always could."

"Charlie, I'm happy. Is that really that bad?"

"No, it's not. And I *am* glad that Lori's convinced you to reconnect, I just don't want you to get yourself hurt. *We* didn't work out, but I *do* care for you. Promise me that if she tries getting you to do anything you don't feel comfortable with you'll say no, OK?"

I frown. "She's not like that. She won't try to *force* me to do anything. What's brought all this chameleon stuff on, anyway? You've never mentioned it before."

"I kinda wondered about it before, but...I just realised something, that's all."

"What?"

"Well, when I mentioned the PVC thing, you..."

"I, what?" I prompt, and immediately start to regret it.

"I could see it on your face. You weren't entirely opposed to the idea."

My cheeks start to flush, and my mouth drops open in shock, unable to form a smart-ass retort. Hell, I can't even manage a stupid-ass retort at this point.

Charlie laughs, and it's a long, whooping laugh that spills into her words. "It's a good job that she thinks you're cute when you're embarrassed because you are *so* going to be blushing a lot when you two get out of first gear."

"Gee, thanks," I groan. With all the amusement I'm giving people lately, I'm beginning to wonder if I should consider switching careers and becoming a stand-up. I glance over at the clock on the wall. It's a hybrid model that works with modern digital tech but built to resemble an old pendulum piece. They're all the rage right now, or so I'm told. From the way the video display just jumped, I think Charlie's might be broken. A quick check of my phone confirms that the time is right, at least.

"I better head out," I say, getting to my feet. "And your pendulum just jumped, by the way. You may want to get that checked out."

"Oh, it does that." Charlie smiles, rising to walk me to the door. "I've had it checked over three times now and there's no faults. It keeps the right time, so I'll forgive it a few little visual blips."

"Thanks, Charlie. It's been a fun afternoon."

"It really has. And don't worry too much about the chameleon thing, I *am* half joking. I don't expect you to be having the Tech Shift op any time soon, at least. Although...they do say that everyone starts to resemble their pets, right?"

"*Diu,*" I groan.

LORI MUST HAVE been keeping an eye out for me. I know this because she opened the door to her bungalow a few seconds after I stepped out of the cab and onto Forster Street, New Hopeland's little slice of white-picket-fence America. I'm not complaining, though. I may not be through my new relationship jitters yet, but it's nice to know that my company is something *someone* looks forward to. The majority of the people I spend any real time with are strictly on a work basis, and if you're coming to investigate, then it's safe to say that things are already a long way from being skookum. Show me someone who gets excited about that sort of meeting and I'll show you a masochist.

As I reach the door, Lori leans in to meet me with a quick peck on the cheek. "I've got something to show you," she says and glides back into the hallway, her loose-fit T-shirt swishing quietly as it follows the movement.

"I'm great, thanks for asking," I tease, pulling the door shut behind me. "And how have you been? Good? Good."

Lori laughs from somewhere in the living room and replies, "I hope you're in the mood for coffee."

"Always." I lean casually against the door frame. "How'd you manage to get *that* ready so quickly?"

"I got one of those new temperature-maintaining boxes from the adverts." She hands me a hot mug of caffeinated liquid joy. "This is about half an hour old."

I take a tentative sip and let out a surprised *huh*. "This is pretty good."

"Isn't it? The thing works kinda like a microwave. As long as what you put in is around the right temperature to begin with, the power consumption is low too. You just tell it what you're putting in and how hot you want it, and it keeps checking the temperature and maintains a constant with intermittent blasts."

"So, what happens if you put something in that isn't at the right temperature yet?"

Lori shrugs. "According to the instructions, it gets confused and overheats."

I laugh, take another sip of coffee, and lower myself onto the two-seater couch next to the door. "Sounds like a serious design flaw to me."

"That's actually the second cup that I made too," Lori replies, nodding towards my drink as she sits down next to me. "The mug itself ended up boiled on the first one. The troubleshooters said it was something to do with polar molecules or air bubbles in the ceramic. These ones seem fine. Still, it's pretty cool as a novelty item."

"Useful too." I frown, noticing the slightly screwed-up piece of paper that Lori has wedged between her hand and the mug handle. "What's that?"

"Ooh, that's what I wanted to show you." She grabs the paper with her free hand and places her mug on the floor. She smooths the paper out, revealing an A5 sized flyer, and holds it out to me. I follow suit with my mug and take the printout, focusing instinctively on the bold lettering near the bottom of the page.

"Kitsune?" I ask, raising a quizzical eyebrow. "As in fox?"

Lori smiles and nods. "Exactly. They do interpretive dance and spoken word performances based on Japanese folklore."

That sounds about right. The flyer is for a run of live shows starting tomorrow night and is almost entirely taken up by a single photo of a figure wearing a traditional Japanese kimono and a white fox mask with red detailing. It isn't a million miles away from something that you'd see during a "festival" episode of an anime. If my memory is right, the thickness of the obi keeping the garment closed, and the length of the sleeve extension, is feminine in style, as is the space between the collar and the person's neck. The way the kimono hides the person's natural build makes it hard to tell if they're actually female or a male taking on the role as they would in a traditional kabuki show.

The composition of the photo is good at drawing attention to the subtler details. First, the kimono looks beautifully made. I don't know whether it's a photo from an actual performance, or whether it was set up specifically for the advertising, but the lighting has been set to catch the shine of the intricately stitched patterning on the outfit. In this case, it depicts a cherry blossom tree in full bloom with a kitsune spirit sitting against the base of the tree. The second thing I notice is that the lone figure has twisted their body to splay nine white tails with red tips out behind them, making the still image far more dynamic and mobile. The tails are pouring out from a gap just under the obi sash, meaning that the kimono must have been either modified or purpose-built to accommodate the appendages. Finally, in a break from the otherwise traditional feel of the performer, the mask's mouth is wide open with a full row of teeth and a vaguely realistic looking tongue lolling out. The slight shine to both the mask and the artfully positioned clawed hands peeking out from the kimono sleeves give away that they're made of the same metal as Lori's panther suit, Ink, which means that this particular kitsune is a Tech Shifter.

Charlie was right earlier when she said I wouldn't be going through that particular op any time soon. The process basically involves a row of rubber-tipped plugs being inserted into your head and spine, allowing you to wear and control what are essentially overly complicated animal costumes. The problem is, I was there when the first Tech Shifters emerged into New Hopeland, and I lived through the initial turmoil that it caused. At the start, three groups of people took up the role. They became known as the Three F's: Furries, Fetishists, and Freaks. The first two groups were just out for some fun which, given the nature of the operation, still seems a bit excessive to me, but hey, to each their own. The problem was the third group. That's where the infamous TS Murder Files came from. Yup, giving the city's unhinged their own custom-built werewolf suits was just plain stupid. Things are more robust now, though. Full psych tests are carried out before a surgeon will even consider you for the operation, which prevents more Freaks from getting through. It also means that the law enforcement agencies are comfortable enough to run their own TS units.

Lori is a second F, though she doesn't like the term. For her, Tech Shifting is a way to blow off steam, and while petplay like that is technically associated with the BDSM community, there's nothing sexual in it for her, so she isn't fond of being viewed as a Fetishist. Since I started dating Lori, I've learned a lot more about Tech Shifting in general, though the memories of the early days still freak me out a little. The ones that caused the trouble were mostly anthropomorphic hybrids like the one on the flyer too, which kinda sets me on edge. But this is the first time I've seen Tech Shift gear with a human haircut; the person in the photo has flowing, silver hair swaying in synch with the tails. The way the ears peek out from under it is actually kinda cute.

Lori laughs, drawing me out of my internal monologue. "What?" I ask.

"I knew it. This is why you need this. You're never off the clock."

I glare at her, not because I'm upset at all, but because...well, glaring is as natural to me as smiling is to most people. A shrink would probably tell me that it's a defence mechanism thrown up when I think I'm about to get verbally attacked, but there's no truth in that. Or that's what I tell myself anyway. Usually with a scowl.

"Never off the clock? What are you talking about? I'm not working right now."

"Of course you are. C'mon, Cassie, I can read you like an open book. Your face gives it away. The subtle way your eyes flick across the page, the slight on-off tightening at the corners of your mouth. You're studying the picture for clues. What for, I don't know, but you're definitely doing it."

I'd protest but, much to my chagrin, she's right. I guess it's because all I've had up until recently was work. Even when I didn't have a case on, I was still trawling through the local news sites to see if I could get a head start on anything that may have been about to come my way. The problem is, PI work in New Hopeland has peaks and troughs, and it's near impossible to predict when each will happen. As it is, the press I received when I solved Lori's case the month before last has led to a near-constant influx of work. The same thing happened when I found Jonah Burrell's daughter, and before that when I helped recover the arms that an upstart street gang had lifted from a visiting military team. Since there's no real way to tell when it's all gonna bottom out again, I've been taking on everything that comes my way, just in case I'm about to hit another dry spell. All of the focus on work has meant that, recently at least, my mind hasn't been entirely *here* when I've been with Lori.

"Remind me never to play poker with you," I groan. "So, how many are there in the troupe?"

"Just the one."

"One? Didn't you say *they*?"

"Yup. In folklore, kitsune were shapeshifters and could take on any gender, so this kitsune does the same. They use voice changers and alter their body language depending on what they're depicting, and they use neutral pronouns. Honestly, I wouldn't be surprised if, under all the gear, they identified outside the binary."

"Huh. So what F do you think they are?"

"I couldn't tell you. Is that what you were trying to figure out?"

I nod. "Given that it's at the biggest show venue in the city, I figured they weren't a secret third F. I remember you saying that pretty much all second Fs are petplayers too, so setting up a job linked to Tech Shifting would be counterproductive for that. You also said that most second Fs used a full animal suit and that it was the first Fs who went for the hybrid style, so I was thinking they're probably a Furry."

Lori lets out an exasperated sigh and throws her arms out in defeat. "Okay, okay, I'll bite. You're not gonna let yourself shut down otherwise. First, I definitely agree about them not being a secret Freak. They've been around for a few years and Freaks tend to be a little too unstable to not get caught, even if they manage to control themselves long enough to make it through testing. As far as the Fetishist thing goes, *most* go full animal but not *all*. Also, you're basing your thinking on the idea that the world they're trying to escape is itself a job. My reasons are my own, and not everyone has the same stressors that I do. For all we know, they could have, I dunno, disabled relatives to care for, and this gives them a way to fund said responsibilities while removing themselves from it for a time. Or they could have been bullied as a kid. This could be a way for them to take a step back and be someone else, or, more importantly, someone that other people love rather than ridicule.

"Yes, the gear makes it *more likely* that they're a Fur, but it doesn't guarantee it. You haven't actually met any TS Furs, have you?" I shake my head, and she continues, "The majority go for cute designs. That means straight up cartoony or quirky horror. This is traditional in style, which doesn't really fit in with that. Of course, whether the design was made to fit in with the job, or the job evolved *from* the style, is anybody's guess. Now, Miss Detective, can you guess what all that means?"

I roll my eyes. "That I'm overthinking something unimportant and that I'll never know the answers anyway."

"Exactly."

"It's an interesting concept," I say, and Lori pounces on the opening.

"*I* thought so. The thing is, my boss got a couple of freebie tickets for tomorrow and the next day. It isn't really his sort of thing, and they only need reporters to cover *one* of the nights. He thought that night two would be better as it'll give Kitsune a chance to sort out any technical faults that pop up, so that left opening night going free and...well...I agreed to take them off his hands. So, what do you say? I could give you one ticket and pretend I got it because I can't tell the difference between Chinese and Japanese folklore, and you can give me the other ticket and pretend that you think I'll enjoy it because I'm a Tech Shifter and must, therefore, love all things Tech Shift related."

"Seriously? You want us to pretend to be bigots for a night out?"

Lori laughs, and it's one of her full-bodied laughs that makes her whole body shake in mirth. She grabs me into a hug and presses her face to my shoulder, tears rolling down her cheeks as she says, "Of course not. It makes more sense than questioning every little thing about a photo of someone dressed as an anthropomorphic fox spirit, though."

"Okay, okay," I reply, joining the laughter. "Point taken. It *is* pretty hard to switch off as of late."

Lori steps back and looks up at me, wiping the tears away from her pale blue eyes. "Honestly, the whole thing sounds kinda hammy to me, but you never know. At worst, we'll either get a surprisingly good show or something we can laugh about later."

I tilt my head and let my eyes relax into a warm curiosity. "This is really important to you, isn't it?"

Lori blinks and turns her face away, her cheeks reddening a little. "You are an incredible person, but you really don't look after yourself sometimes. I have Ink, but you don't really have many ways to wind down and get out of that work headspace." She lifts her head back to mine, and her eyes are a beautiful mix of pleading and something else hidden just beneath the surface. For someone who spends part of her time as a large cat, she sure does puppy-dog eyes well. "Please, Cassie, let me take care of you with this."

"Okay," I sigh. "Okay, I'll go. But for the record, there are nine-tailed fox stories in Chinese folklore too. We called them *jiuweihu*."

"Good to know," she says, and pulls me into another hug. "Thank you."

Confidence. It was confidence lurking beneath the cuteness. She knew I couldn't resist *that* look. I'd cry foul by way of manipulation, but I'm pretty sure she also knew that, deep down, *I* know she's right. At the very least when I'm around *her*. I don't know if I'm focusing on work because the relationship jitters make me so uncomfortable, or if there's still part of me that doesn't feel ready to be with someone, but something has to change. This could be just what I need.

Chapter Two

LOOKING AROUND ME, I'm glad that I opted for one of my few fancier suits. It's not exactly in fashion, but the slightly looser fitting shirt, lack of tie, and almost flowy blazer and trousers mean that I don't feel too underdressed among the upmarket crowd the show has drawn. Okay, so it *is* something that I used to wear at the jazz clubs when Charlie and I went out, but it still fits, and it's probably the most classy-looking thing I own, so that's okay, right? Charlie didn't mention it when I ran it by her, so that's a good sign that I'm not making some dating faux pas. Or I hope it is, anyway. I'm still far too out of practice with this stuff.

Lori laughed at the outfit being relatively similar to my work gear, but she complimented me too, so I'll take that as a positive, even if it did make me blush like an embarrassed teenager. Her own silken blue dress is stunning and gives away that she knows how to dress for this sort of thing far better than I do. Who knew that someone with what is essentially a metal mohawk could look delicate? Or is it more that she normally has a harder look to her, and this is simply more feminine in comparison...? *Night out, night out, night out. Stop the overthinking, relax, and do something about those sweaty palms.*

I wipe my hands on my trouser legs, stealthily of course, and hunt for a conversation starter to distract myself with. I settle on, "I think this might be the first time I've been inside the central theatre."

"Really? That surprises me. It's one of the bigger tourist grabbers in the city. I thought that most citizens had been to at least one show here, even if it was just to see what all the fuss was about."

I shrug. "It never really appealed. I mean, the outside's nice in that old style picturesque sorta way, but there weren't any shows on that made me want to pay to come in. I'm kinda regretting it now, though. The hybrid architecture is incredible."

Lori smiles and leads me to a staircase that winds up towards the main show floor in a classical mansion style. What sets it apart from the other traditional architecture I've seen is that the steps themselves are patterned with grass that actually bends underfoot. I think I heard a gentle crunch too. To add to the effect, the handrail is patterned like winding vines and branches, decorated with intermittent flowers. It looks real, and sounds real, but I can feel the actual shape of the thing is as flat as you'd expect.

Noticing my embarrassingly enthralled gaze, Lori says, "Pretty, isn't it? They've got video projection equipment built in but covered in a solid touch-sensitive layer. That's how it knows to animate the grass bending underfoot. If you look closely at the railings, any time your hand gets near a bug, it'll scamper off."

I glance down at my hand and see a ladybird speeding into a hole between two vines. "Wow..."

"Want to know something cooler?" I nod, and Lori continues, "This display is custom. Every time they do a show, they consult with the performers to build something suitable to link in with the act. It's to help create a sense of immersion."

"Come here often?" I ask and throw in an awkward wink at the jokey chat-up line.

"Nah," Lori giggles. "This is only my...fifth time, I think."

"So, you just take an interest in how it all works, eh?"

"Nope. I'll let you in on a secret. I've performed here."

"Really?" I ask, stopping in my tracks and giving Lori a quizzical look.

"Don't get too excited," she replies, beckoning me on. "I took drama back in high school, and part of the course meant that we had to put on a professional show. The school managed to get this place booked for the evening, and I got to see the production side in action. Watching the camera team was part of what sparked my interest in photography, actually."

I shake my head sadly and sigh. "I have led such a boring life."

"Of course you have, Miss Punches-The-Villains. It wasn't a big deal, anyway. I was an extra. Background dancer number two, or something like that. My parents were proud, though, so that was something."

We settle into our seats and I say, "I think that's the first time you've mentioned your parents. Are they...?"

"Oh, they're still with us. They retired to Australia way back. Can you guess which part?"

"Uh... Brisbane? Melbourne?"

"Hopeland, would you believe? It's part of Queensland."

"I never knew there was a Hopeland in Australia."

"Neither did I until they moved there. It's all nice and rural apparently, virtually untouched by all this modern stuff. My dad calls it Old Hopeland."

"That's a shame, in a way."

"How so?"

"It means they miss out on the balance. I mean, look at this place. The building is structured like something from the late 1900s, but everything's integrated. The metal security shutters are painted up to look like windows. The stairs are old in design but covered in tech that's been set to mimic a nature scene, solely for this show. The seats are the old-style fold-down ones but with modern comfort specifications. The stage is a classic semi-circle with big curtains, but I bet that's got modern features too, right?"

Lori tilts her head towards the stage, trying to remember. "Yeah, actually. The back wall is built the same as the stairs. It means you don't need handmade sets unless you *want* to go old school."

"See? Traditional look, traditional arts, but modern sensibilities. Past and future intertwined. When you think about it, this place is like a physical representation of what New Hopeland was *supposed* to be."

"It's scary, but I can't figure out whether you love the city or are just very disappointed with it."

"I love *the potential* of the place, I guess. It amazes me what can be achieved when humans put their mind to it. It's also amazing to think that it tends to be artists who manage it. Not bad for a group that usually get described as either dreamers or layabouts, is it? It makes you wonder why most of the ever-so-sensible, not to mention highly paid, politicians can't get the balance right. Sometimes, I wonder if we should give the city to the starving artists and demote the lawmakers to a purely advisory role."

"I think that someone's a secret anarchist."

"Down with the establishment," I chuckle, just as the lights begin to lower and the first sounds of a shamisen cue up over the speakers.

GIVEN MY OWN uncertainty over what to expect, I have to hand it to Kitsune. While I doubt that we were the only ones here who weren't lifelong fans, the vast majority of the audience was buzzing by show time. And I can't say I blame them. I was too by the end of it. Things started with the curtains sliding aside, accompanied by the sound of a shamisen playing over the speakers. From there, Kitsune danced delicately onto the stage, twisting and turning with the well-practised movements of a vaguely familiar traditional dance, while the back screen led us through the passing of the four seasons in a woodland. As the music drew to a close, Kitsune moved to the front of the stage and, using a silken, if slightly mechanical-tinged, female voice welcomed us to the show.

"Those in attendance have done my siblings and I a great favour, for it is those who come to visit that give us the means to live. The kitsune are known to be wily tricksters, but we are not without honour, and we *always* repay a favour given to us. Perhaps then we can repay that which you have bestowed upon us with some entertainment. Come, and we shall help you forget the troubles of the day, if only for a little while."

And so began what turned out to be a wonderfully enjoyable variety show. Most of the evening was given over to storytelling, with Kitsune playing a variety of different fox spirits as they told their tales as first-person accounts, complete with a variety of scenic backdrops. Oh, and the delicately woven silk pattern on the kimono? I'm not sure how they did it, but each different *sibling* had their own design, and it changed in the blink of an eye, without the need for Kitsune to exit the stage. My best guess is that each design was created by a tech team with military precision on their projection aim.

As for the stories themselves, some of them were genuinely funny, such as the one where a carefree young fox stumbled upon a proud, boastful samurai and set about taking him down a peg or two through sheer trickery and guile. My favourite was a heartwarming story of a young child who found a kitsune that had been hurt by a local farmer and nursed it back to health. As a thank you, the kitsune followed the boy through his life and provided assistance at the times he needed it most. This culminated in the fox leading the then old man's spirit away from a hungry demon and on to the afterlife.

Then there was the finale.

A full light and video show was given over to the story of the fox maiden who fell in love with a hardworking fisherman. The fox admired the man from afar and found herself drawn not only to the way that he diligently carried out his work but the kindness with which he treated others. Taking the form of a human woman, the fox orchestrated a meeting one evening and, after a whirlwind romance, they were married. Unfortunately, tragedy struck soon after. The fisherman, recounting his memories of the wedding day to a friend, described a sun shower, or rain falling from a clear sky. He spoke of the woodland animals that had come to watch from the outskirts of the ceremony, with foxes, in particular, outnumbering the human guests two-to-one. This, his friend had told him, sounded like a *kitsune no yomeiri*, or fox wedding, that he had heard about in one of his grandmother's tales. Though such an event usually only applied to the marriage of two kitsune, the resemblance in description was uncanny.

Concerned, and slightly drunk, the fisherman returned home and confronted his wife. Loving him so dearly, the kitsune revealed herself to him and, though he did not fear her, the fisherman was disgusted that she had lied to him for so long and demanded that she leave. He never remarried, and never knew that the fox maiden was pregnant when he kicked her out. "This," Kitsune said, "was how *we* came to be. Our father is now long dead, but his blood lives on in each of us who have visited you tonight. And so, with this bittersweet tale and one final dance, our debt to you is repaid."

Finally, Kitsune reeled across the stage, the ever-shrinking spotlight illuminating the different designs that appeared on their kimono. With each new image, the performer subtly changed their body language, allowing the audience one final glimpse of each character that had been featured. In the end, the Kitsune from the flyer appeared and, with a gracious bow, dimmed the spotlight to pitch black.

The standing ovation was well deserved.

AS WE'RE FILING out, Lori grips my hand, and I say, "You are absolutely terrible."

"What did *I* do?" she giggles, knowing full well what I'm talking about.

"When the fisherman kicked his fox wife out. You waited until everyone went quiet, then leaned in and whispered, 'It's a good job you already know I'm a panther, isn't it?' You knew that I'd struggle not to laugh."

Lori squeezes my hand again and gives me a cheeky grin. "What can I say? I saw an opportunity and I took it."

"Uh-huh. Well, I'll have you know, I see things too. Like how you were welling up when he kicked her out. You so did that to stop yourself crying."

Lori stops then, and I end up walking a few steps past her before realising. When I turn, the smile she has on is a sad one.

"You're easily embarrassed, and you slip up sometimes, but not everyone is as accepting as you, Cassie. Try to remember that."

And with that, she resumes her walk. Being as dense as I am, it takes a moment to realise what she meant. "Someone left you because of Ink?"

"So, how did you find it?" Lori asks, ignoring my question.

I sigh and make a mental note to think before I speak more often. Or at the very least, to speak to Jane before I put my foot in it some more.

"Honestly? I was really surprised. I'm tempted to see if there are any shows available on download. What about you?"

"Less hammy than I expected, but a little too cheesy for my tastes. If you enjoyed it, though, then that's good enough for me. Getting you to relax and not think about work for a bit was more than worth it."

I take Lori's hand this time and give it a tight squeeze. "Thank you, Lori," I say, and the warm smile that rises on her face is better than anything I saw on stage. *It goes deeper than the smiles I saw when I was working her case. It's warmer, more content.*

We're about to leave through the main doors when a man in a suit comes running up to us. "Excuse me. Sorry, but are you Cassandra Tam? The private investigator?"

I turn to face the man and frown. "I prefer Cassie or Caz, but yes."

"Ah, good. Kitsune thought that they recognised you. You were in the fifth row, right?"

"Good eyes," Lori says. "The audience lights were off."

The man shrugs. "Fox spirits, right? Look, I know that it's a bit cheeky given you were here for a show and all, but Kitsune would really like to speak with you." He turns to Lori and adds, "They said that they saw the two of you holding hands and that you're welcome to come along too."

"Wow," Lori replies. "Well, now I feel totally spied on."

"I'm so sorry."

I sigh and turn to Lori. "What do you think?"

"I think this is going to completely negate the idea of this being a work-free evening. You probably *should* go, though. I'll come too, if that's okay If nothing else, you still owe me some evening, even if we spend it working."

I nod and look back to the man. "Lead the way."

KITSUNE'S CHANGING ROOM is pretty small by celebrity standards. Looking around, I can see a long, leather couch against one wall. There's a mid-sized table containing a fruit basket and a bottle of water in the middle of the room and, flanked by a couple of armchairs, a television by the door. A mirrored desk stands opposite the couch and a fold-out panel screen near the back wall. It looks like there's some clothing hanging over the top of the screen, but I can't tell what. At a push, I'd guess a plain top and a pair of jeans. Like I said, small by celebrity standards.

The room is also well lit. There's a nice, stain-free carpet on the floor, and not one speck of dirt is visible anywhere, so celebrities clearly haven't quite fallen to my level of living just yet. That's a big, high-earning thumbs-up to the human obsession with other people's lives, eh?

I thrive in clutter, I remind myself and move my gaze back to the couch. Stretched out...no, make that luxuriating, on said couch is Kitsune, still in their mask and kimono. While the mask retains its markings, the kimono is in a state that the theme park performers of the past would refer to as "breaking the magic." Yes, it's still tied and worn with the same elegance as during the live show, but the markings are gone. Instead, several runs of small black nodules are protruding from the fabric like some sort of bizarre dead LED pockmarks. I'd wonder what they are, but I've seen them before; they're short-range holographic projectors. Way back when I was choosing Bert's design, the store had a bunch of them set up in a cube layout so they could show me a 3D representation of his final shape. Kitsune must have them set up so that the stagehands can alter the design as and when they change characters.

The man in the suit, who we have learned is named Mr. Smitt, clears his throat, and a quiet yawn drifts out from Kitsune's muzzle, but their eyes don't open. "I have Cassandra Tam for you, and her partner, Miss Redwood. Miss Tam prefers Cassie or Caz, and Miss Redwood is not giving a first name." Smitt pauses, then adds, in a gentler tone, "Did you want me to stick around?"

Kitsune opens a relaxed eye and glances over towards Lori and me. "No, no, it's all right, Kevin. If you could just make sure that we aren't disturbed, that would be fantastic." Kevin Smitt nods in response and leaves the room. Kitsune sits up and grabs the bottle of water from the table. "Drink? I'm afraid that I only have water. They don't allow anything else other than tea and coffee back here and I'm afraid that, since the Tech Shift operation, I've been displaying some mild allergic symptoms to caffeine."

It's interesting. Even without the vocal filters, Kitsune's voice is very light, but it doesn't give away a specific gender any more than their promotional photos do. Thanks to years of hard work, I'm pretty close to Andrew Hoover, the Captain of the local PD, and I've had the pleasure of meeting various members of his family over that time. He has a nephew, Jimmy, who has a similar way of talking, at least when he's not ramping up the machismo in an effort to placate his father. Jimmy has a definite male edge to his voice, though, while Kitsune doesn't. The mask muffles their accent too, though I think that it may have a hint of Japanese to it. But that could be my mind trying to rationalise the voice with the cultural connotations of the show.

"I'm fine," I reply, and Kitsune looks back to Lori. Lori shakes her head, and Kitsune waves us to the armchairs. "I'm sorry, but did you want to get changed before we speak? We'd be happy to leave the room while you get ready. It must be hard work performing in both the TS gear and a kimono thick enough to house projectors without them moving out of line with each other, even if they are the smaller, lightweight models."

"You don't know the half of it," Kitsune sighs. "There's a wireless motion detection system in each hand too," they add, waving two metallic, clawed paws. "You'll note that my tails are missing. They don't yet make multi-tailed suits, you see, and the number is important within the folklore, so we had to find other solutions. The projector tucked under the obi sash keeps the back open nicely, and it allows movement, both in animation and in the actual device, but it's a bit stronger than the main ones."

"Meaning that it's heavier," I reply.

"Indeed. The way the system works is identical to the tail guidance in regular suits though."

I frown, and Lori clarifies, "Regular Tech Shift gear uses two small wireless touchpads to control tails, one for the bottom half, and one for the top half. They're embedded in the hand rest of Ink's front legs. For hybrid-style gear, they usually sit inside the thumb of each hand. It's the same concept in each one, but animal-style gear allows for bigger movements, while hybrid gear measures micro movements."

"Which would be rather fiddly, given the level of movement that I require. These are built into the paw pads and are set to register larger movements so that the tails can move in time with the different dance routines and my more flamboyant gestures," Kitsune explains, demonstrating one of the hand flourishes from the show. They pause then and chuckle. "Ah, but I'm rambling. I am afraid that changing is, contractually speaking, impossible. Will my appearance be a problem?"

"No, I'm used to Tech Shifters..."

Lori laughs and cuts in with, "You are *so* not used to us yet."

I laugh quietly, despite myself. The miserable old loner that still lives in my head says I should be angry about that; I'm working after all. But the part of me that was enjoying the evening is far more prominent and reminds me that this was supposed to be Lori's evening too. I can allow her a small jab or two on that basis. "My early experiences with Tech Shifters were *not* positive," I say, addressing Kitsune. "I'm getting better, though. What do you mean by 'contractually speaking,' if you don't mind me asking?"

"Not at all. It is essentially as it sounds. The Kitsune brand is a joint venture between myself and Kevin, and there is a lot of paperwork involved dealing with how the whole thing is to be played out in every mundane situation that you could imagine. What it means is that I can boss Kevin about and make him my dogsbody as much as is required, but at the same time, I must respect his rather brilliant marketing strategies. Part of that means that the mystery of the Kitsune's true identity is to be protected at all times. As such, I do not meet with anyone without my *professional* face on. It seems a little strange, I know, but he was previously a historian of certain old-world sporting brands by trade and thought that applying a degree of what he called *kayfabe* would help give the whole thing a new edge. I can't say that he was wrong."

"So, are you Kitsune when you're around family too?" Lori asks. "Or partners?"

"Oh, I have no time for partners, not with *my* touring schedule. With family, I can be myself, though Kevin did insist upon them signing a gagging order to prevent them from revealing my identity to anyone who hadn't signed a similar contract. You should have seen my mother's face when he brought that up. I honestly thought that the rolling pin she was holding was going to be put to nefarious use. Outside Kevin, even my oldest friends do not know who resides beneath the mask."

"That must be hard to maintain," I say.

"Oh yes, I have cover stories and everything. It's somewhat akin to witness protection if television is to be believed. As far as most know, I am simply a touring stagehand for the great performing fox spirit."

I nod. "Kitsune, as pleasant as this is, I assume there was a reason that you wanted to see me?"

"Oh yes, of course. I saw the news coverage of your recent success with that Gary Locke character," they say, and Lori flinches slightly. "As far as local detectives go, there are plenty of them about, but you are certainly the most well regarded. I have actually been in town for a week now, and I am due to remain here for a further two. I am afraid that, over that initial period, I was subject to a crime of the nature I am led to believe the police do not take overly seriously."

"The police wouldn't be happy about not knowing your identity, regardless of the crime. If it's one that they won't usually touch, that doesn't leave many possibilities. What are we talking about?"

"It is rather lonely on the road," they sigh wistfully. "A few months ago, we stopped in Toledo, and I was awoken from a post-performance nap by a clattering outside the tour bus. I wandered out, expecting to find a fan or two hunting autographs, and instead found this charming little thing skulking around the bins. I named him Fish."

Kitsune produces a phone from their kimono, loads up a photo, and passes it over. It shows a snow white American Shepherd dog sitting on one of the tour bus seats and giving the camera a suspicious look. It's too big to be a puppy, but certainly not big enough to be fully grown.

"You named your dog Fish?"

"It seems strange, doesn't it?" Kitsune laughs. "There's a reason, though." They take the phone back and enlarge the picture, revealing that the dog's tail is about half the length it should be. It was easy to miss at normal size because the single colouring made it seem like it was tucked under its legs. "When I was young, my parents had some rosetail betta fish. One of them was pure white, and it had a habit of nibbling through its tail fin. When we took Fish to the vet, they said that the tail damage, judging by the angle of the marks, was likely self-inflicted. I couldn't remember what my parents called the fish, so I just stuck with Fish."

I nod. "And I assume that Fish is now missing?"

"I am afraid so. It happened yesterday, during the early hours. I was woken by a loud bang and found that Fish was gone, and the tour bus door was open."

"Could Fish have run away?"

"It would have been difficult for him to open the door, but not impossible. I don't think that he would have run, though. We were lifelines for each other, you see. He kept me company during the day, and when he had nightmares, I comforted him. If he was spooked, he would usually run and hide near my bed. I heard something else too, a van door being slammed shut maybe? And then an engine."

"So you're thinking that he was stolen."

"Honestly? I don't know. Do you think that you could take the case? How much would it cost?"

"Cost is a difficult one with cases like this, because it depends on time and what's involved. To give you an example, I found a missing cat last week, and the case cost the owner $500. A few weeks before that, a missing dog case took a lot longer and led me into a fight with an idiot who was stealing dogs for breeding. That cost $1,000."

"Well, what if I was to offer a flat fee of $10,000? That would be regardless of whether you found Fish in a day or two weeks. If you can't find him before I leave, I'll have to accept that he simply isn't built for family living, and you'll get the same fee."

"That's a lot of money for this sort of case."

"Cassie, was it?" Kitsune asks, and I nod. "If that is true, then it should tell you how important Fish is to me."

I rest my elbows on my knees and drop my chin into my hands. It *is* a lot of money, and I don't want to screw Kitsune over. At the same time, with the number of jobs I've had recently, there's no telling how much time I'd be able to throw into it if comparatively bigger cases keep coming.

"Sorry," Lori says, "but is there somewhere I could speak to Cassie privately for a moment?"

Kitsune tilts their head curiously but says, "Of course. There's a door behind the screen. That leads to the bathroom. Is something wrong?"

"Not in the way that you think," Lori replies and pushes up to her feet. "Cassie, come with me."

I frown but follow Lori anyway. If there's one thing I've learned in the near two months we've been dating, it's that Lori doesn't try to get me alone for a chat unless she's genuinely worried about something, and then, it's usually because she's spotted something I haven't. Probably about me. We make our way into a bathroom about the size of my living room and Lori pushes the door shut and asks, "Kitsune's offer. What do you think about it?"

"I'm thinking that it's too much money, but that they're so serious about it they probably won't back down on it. That's *if* I take the case."

"So it *is* an if. Why wouldn't you take it?"

I cross my arms defensively and reply, "Because I'm getting a lot of cases through the door right now, meaning that I probably won't be able to dedicate enough time to it to do a good job. For that sort of money, I wouldn't feel comfortable with that."

"You told me a while back that missing pet cases are usually pretty easy though. Even that one with the breeder was quick compared to some cases you've had."

"Yeah, but I was in a brief lull at the time. And they were being charged my normal rate. This is...uncomfortable for the type of case."

"OK, so say you turned the case down. What sort of cases would you need to come through to you to make as much money in the same time?"

I shrug. "Mid-sized theft, maybe a couple of *simple* missing people cases?"

"And what are you getting coming in right now?"

"A lot of small theft and unfaithful partners."

"Which are all time-consuming and for less return, right?"

I narrow my eyes at Lori. "And your point is?"

"Take this one as an exclusive case. Turn down all the others that come through until it's done and concentrate on this one."

"And why would I want to do that?"

Lori smiles. "Because you need a break. Say you find Fish within a day or two. You get a nice, big payment, and if you feel that you *must* keep going with your insane schedule, then you haven't lost much time. If it takes you the whole two weeks, you'll make more than you would have likely made otherwise. It gives you a chance to relax a little while still bringing money in."

"And if another big case comes my way part way through it? Then what?"

Lori rolls her eyes. "Then you take it. Just turn down the little ones while you're on this one."

I sigh and lean back against the wall next to the disturbingly clean toilet. "I guess I *could* do with a break."

"Good," Lori says and pushes the door open. "She'll take the case," she yells and shoots me a wicked grin while Kitsune starts shouting back their thanks.

My jaw drops open in shock. Lori's argument was sound, but the money is still uncomfortable. Now I really will have to concentrate on Kitsune's case to make myself feel better about accepting it. Lori knew that I might change my mind and just made it so that I can't back out. "I can't...you just..." I whisper-shout.

"Yup," Lori winks. "You can thank me after you find the lost little puppy."

Chapter Three

"WHAT?" I GRUMBLE through a mouthful of half-chewed toast. Bert responds by half closing the metal ring that outlines his eyes, giving the impression that he's narrowing them at me. "You've seen me worse than this."

Bert is a Familiar Unit, which basically means that he's one of a line of mass-produced AIs. While most serve as family-friendly pet substitutes, some are used as glorified guard dogs. In Bert's case, I managed to convince the retailer to give him a mix of both the "Family" and "Protector" programming, meaning that my shiny little bat-winged, beaked gargoyle is what would happen if you had a particularly sarcastic cat that was loyal enough to tackle intruders. Undeterred by my statement, Bert continues to stare, completely unflinching.

"I'm allowed to get annoyed sometimes, Bert."

"Caw," he agrees, but remains in place.

I roll my eyes and throw my toast down in frustration before blurting, "*Ceoi zoeng*, I'm pissed off with Lori, okay? She put me in a position where I not only couldn't turn a case down but couldn't even take any time to think about it either. And worst of all, she thinks I'm going to thank her for it when it's all done."

Bert opens his eye rings slightly and readjusts his wing claspings to the opposite side, leaving the tip of the left one on top of the right. He says nothing and waits patiently from his position at the opposite end of the work-slash-breakfast table.

"Okay, so if it works out, it's good money. A lot of money too for the case type. Maybe, *and I mean maybe*, I *will* thank her for that. But not until we've had a long talk about professional and personal boundaries." I take an angry gulp of coffee because when you're me, you can make anything look angry. "I mean, I'm right, right? The money's good, missing pets are usually easy, but she had no right to put me in that position. Right?"

Bert opens his beak slowly, then lets it clatter shut in response, creating a rattly metallic *clink-clink-clink-clink-clink* sound. Well, that's new.

"Good talk, Bert," I sigh and head to the bedroom to get dressed.

Always one to get the last word in, my favourite little gargoyle waits until I get to the doorway before responding with a rather pleased sounding, "Caw," and heading off to the kitchen to investigate the new oven again.

I'D AGREED TO meet Kitsune a little before lunchtime so that I could pick up some information. Having not been expecting to be dragged into a case on what was supposed to be an evening off, I hadn't brought any Case Tools with me for them to complete. So instead, I'd given them a list of information off the top of my head to get started with but warned them that they'd need to give me their answers in hard copy and then duplicate them on one of my own tools. They had no issue with that, and so, here I am, standing outside a tour bus parked at the back of the theatre. Looking at the scrapings lining its shell, the bus has obviously seen a fair few miles this tour. The lock on the door is surprisingly basic too; no fingerprint scanners, just a simple keypad and key slot combo.

I straighten my tie and give the door a quick rap. Kevin Smitt opens the door, wearing an expression that is far less apologetic and far more irritated than the one he had the last time I saw him. He steps back inside without saying anything. I take that as all the invitation I'm getting and follow him into the bus. "Nice to see you again too," I grump, sliding the door shut.

"I'm going to need some signatures," Kevin replies, shoving a small wad of papers at me.

"Excuse me?"

Kitsune appears behind Kevin, TS gear in place, but wearing a loose-fitting ensemble of sweater, shirt, and tracksuit bottoms instead of the show kimono. Seeing them towering above the angry manager is a strong reminder of how much height the hybrid-style suits add to a person. Users slip their heels into the digitigrade legs at the point of the suit's ankles, and most of the elongated feet are solid machinery. It's the same in animal-style suits, but because the person wearing it is down lower, the increase doesn't usually register with me. Hybrids, though, pretty much gain another shin's worth, if not more, in height, and it's *very* noticeable.

Kitsune waves me over to a small table and asks, "Do you remember when I said about the waivers that my parents had to sign?" I nod and sigh, seeing where this is going. "Kevin thinks some of the things that you've requested may lead to you learning my true identity."

"Of course they will," Kevin grunts. "Anything that leads to a pre-show CCTV review will show your face." He turns to me then and adds, "I hope you realise how difficult it was to get these set up overnight."

I shrug. "PIs don't just click their fingers and solve cases, Mr. Smitt. It doesn't matter what a client hires me to do, I still need information to operate, and I usually have to figure out what information it is that I need with very little notice. You got your paperwork ready, and I got my list together. Let's call that a small victory and leave it at that. Got a pen?"

"I do," Kitsune replies and leans over Kevin's shoulder to hand me a stick of cheap plastic and ink.

I spend a couple of minutes reading through the waiver, and mentally note the main caveats. If I learn Kitsune's true name, I can't mention it, and I can't reveal that I'm working Kitsune's case, just in case anyone else figures out who they are. There are some other minor things in there about the storage of files relating to the case, but nothing too heavy, so I sign without kicking up any more of a fuss than I find amusing. Sure, there were a couple of scowls and huffs, but you can't blame a girl for enjoying herself.

"Is your partner going to be working the case with you?" Kevin asks.

"We're not *that sort* of partners," I grunt, then add silently, *nor am I talking to her right now.*

"Good," Kevin snaps and retreats to the back of the tour bus.

Kitsune leans back and says, almost musically, "Oh, Kevin, some water would be lovely. Cassie?"

I can see the glint in Kitsune's eyes, and call, "Coffee. Milk, no sugar." From the clanking at the far end of the vehicle, I'm guessing that there's a full kitchenette back there. Fancy. I pull a thick, metal disc out of my pocket and place it on the table. "This is the Case Tool I mentioned. It's equipped with a holo-keypad, and everything that it sends is stored on my private server, so there shouldn't be any security issues. I take it from the waiver that you managed to pull together the stuff I asked for?"

Kitsune nods and hands me a sheet of paper. "The last three tour stops, and a list of places visited here along with dates and, where possible, times. I've noted what I was wearing each day too. It's the same baseball cap each day. It's a simple thing, but it hides the plugs, which helps disguise who I am. As to where we were parked when Fish went missing, that was here."

Kevin returns and places a glass of water with a long straw in front of Kitsune. He places my coffee far less delicately in front of me and pulls over a spare chair, purely so that he can cross his arms and glare at me from a more comfortable position.

"Is there a problem, Mr. Smitt?"

"I'm just at a loss as to why I've had to go to so much bother. Could you not have done all this without the need for so much sensitive information?"

"Sure. I could take a photo and go door to door. You never know, if Kitsune is right about Fish being stolen, maybe seeing me on their doorstep will cause the dognappers to have an attack of conscience and just give him back. That's if they live locally. I suppose I could traipse through every surrounding city too, just to be sure, though. Does that sound reasonable?"

"Yes."

I take a mouthful from my mug and say, "I'm glad your coffee making is better than your attitude. If you honestly think that's the way I go about my work, then you haven't read up on me enough. If Fish running away was likely, then door to door would be my first step. Given what Kitsune told me, digging deeper makes more sense. Try to think about it like your paperwork. You take the time to do the legal stuff because that's what it takes to protect the Kitsune brand. I do the digging because that's what it takes to do a thorough job."

"Fine. Do whatever you want, Detective, we're certainly paying you enough." Kevin gets up and storms out of the tour bus, grumbling loudly, but incoherently to himself.

"Don't mind him," Kitsune says. "When Fish disappeared, Kevin actually went running out to see what was going on. I think he's worried about the poor little fluffball too."

"Did he see the van you mentioned?"

"No, I am afraid that it was long gone by then. If he thinks of anything, though, I'll note it down when I complete the Case Tool."

"Good." I nod. "That may be useful."

"So, what happens now?"

"Now, I go for a walk and see what cameras I'm going to need warrants for."

THAT KITSUNE ONLY gave me one sheet of paper let me know pretty quickly they didn't go to too many places during the week-long buildup to the show. As it stands, their excursions into the main city ran like clockwork. The morning hours were blank, which I'm guessing was due to sleep and any regular routine they have. After that, they took Fish for a walk around the local park at around 11:00 p.m. That was followed by a trip to Cartwright's, a dog-friendly cafe a few blocks from Main Street. Much like the morning walk, that was around 11:30 every morning, without variation. After that, it was back to the theatre for rehearsals, meetings, and equipment checks until 5:00 a.m., when Kitsune would do another quick walk around the block with Fish while Kevin sorted out some food.

The area around the theatre will have a few CCTV cameras set up, so that shouldn't be too hard to track. Cartwright's will be more difficult. That whole block is in the low crime zone, so not many buildings have cameras set up. Why does it sound familiar, though? I don't go out that way often.

I sigh and start walking around the theatre building. There's one camera set up near to the tour bus, so that'll be one warrant unless I can get Kitsune or Kevin to convince them to give me access. It looks like there are cameras on each side of the building too, so depending on which way the van went, that could be useful. I start making my way towards the park, keeping an eye out for any potentially useful cameras on display while I wait for a couple of traffic signals to change. It's not until I'm halfway there that I realise I haven't confirmed which way Kitsune walked to the park. *Stupid Cassie.* I pull my phone out. I try the shared cell that lives in the tour bus because that's the only phone number I could get for Kitsune, but it rings through to voice mail.

"Hey, it's Cassie. I just wanted to check which route you took when you walked Fish to the park. I'm guessing it's up by Northfleet Apartments, across the main road, and around by Seventh Son Music on Cross Street. I'll work to that for now, but I won't pester for any footage until you confirm if I'm right."

I hang up. I'm pretty sure that I *am* right. This is the most direct route from the theatre to the park's south entrance. Cartwright's is nearer the north entrance, and it has a direct route back to Cross Street through one of the smaller shopping districts that houses the independent and upstart stores. I should probably have asked Kitsune to confirm if that was their route back too. I guess I'll have to do that when they call back. Until then, I'll stick with logic and intuition. This part of the route at least has a few options for cameras, though I doubt that they'd all capture Kitsune's walk.

The park reminds me a little of Lori. The whole thing is so well maintained by the local government that it seems to have an eternal shine to the thick grass, seemingly untouched by the seasons or weather, despite being entirely real. It's a lot like the grass outside Dean Hollister's office at the top of the local Shift Source Limited building. I doubt I would have ever seen that little piece of unexpected beauty if I hadn't taken Lori's case. She'll be there today, actually, finally taking Hollister up on his offer of a free servicing for Ink. "That's enough distracting yourself." I sigh. "You're angry with her, remember? Work time now."

The inside of the park has a long, winding walk set out that takes you through the entire area, all clearly marked by a decorative stone path. Hollister was right when he said that we shouldn't leave nature behind, but it does stick out against all the tech-covered surroundings. Maybe that's the point. It could be designed to show contrast rather than the balance found in places like the theatre. Regardless, it's not untouched by the hands of progression; there are a handful of tree-mounted cameras surveying the walk. I can't see any pointing towards the open sections, but I can check that with the government offices if I have to.

I leave the park by the north gate, cross the road, and turn onto Dunstone Avenue. It's a nice area. A few trees line either side of the road, though they grow sparser as you get closer to the more typically modern Main Street. In a way, it's kinda like the parkland is stretching out into the surrounding area, but with its fingertips only reaching halfway up the street. Still, Cartwright's at least has a security system in place. The opposite side of the road is residential with no such mod cons on display, so that'll be a door-to-door check at best. Maybe someone saw something, maybe they didn't. There's no way to know just yet.

I turn right at the end of Dunstone and walk through the unmarked run of small stores. Most of them focus on customised or specialist tech supply so, while there's nothing on display, I'd guess they'd have some cameras about. What amazes me with this area is that, while the stores are small in name value, their buildings are pretty big. I think I read somewhere that they're all converted storage units or something. The bigger name brands that came to New Hopeland early on used to pack them out with stock and supplies until their own buildings were suitable for housing or cheaper alternatives could be found. After that, they converted them and started renting them out to up-and-coming types that would either give them a good chance of guaranteed long-term income or potentially prove useful for future deals. In a way, it almost makes the street less of a modern underground market and more of a proving ground.

Cross Street comes into view, and I make the automatic decision to turn left and head towards South Main Street. One way or another, I'm going to need to get some warrants, and since I now can't let the PD know who I'm working for, I'm going to need to file them as being related to an alias. I can't set a fake ID up myself, but I *do* know someone who already owns a few.

"Here's hoping you're in a sharing mood, Devin."

IF THE CENTRAL theatre is a representation of what New Hopeland was *supposed* to be, Devin Carmichael is the perfect representation of the weird moral ambiguity it has embraced. As an assassin for hire, and a damned good one at that, he *should* be one of the bad guys by default. At the same time, though, Devin has his own moral code that he sticks to rigidly, and that means he won't kill indiscriminately. Okay, so he's still a killer, but given the local PD have been known to use him to clean up the messes they can't scrub enough themselves, it's not like he doesn't help to keep the city from falling too far into the dark underbelly that most newcomers stumble across without meaning to.

Devin wasn't in when I knocked earlier, so I treated myself to a much-needed late lunch and a less-needed session of dwelling on how I ended up with this job while I waited for him to materialise. The sun sets early at this time of year, and by the time he finally returns home, the night is beginning to draw in. There's no point heading to the police station now. My usual contacts prefer the early start, early finish shifts and will either be heading home or getting out among the gathering nightlife. The officers that I'm less familiar with take their time with me. I can't blame them for that, but the delay combined with my not yet having heard back from Kitsune would make it harder to get the footage I need, so I may as well wait for the morning.

"Nice view," I say, staring out at the increasingly busy Main Street several stories below his penthouse window.

Devin leans back into his chair and lifts his right leg, resting the ankle across his left knee. He tilts his cowboy hat back and takes a mouthful of bourbon from a pristinely clean, shiny glass, then says in his slow Southern drawl, "It always is, Caz. And ya only ever comment on it when you want something."

I glance back over my shoulder, and he treats me to one of his *charming* smiles that teeters on the dividing line between confidence and arrogance. I say treat because that's how *he* describes the act. With his toned physique and vintage cowboy style, a lot of ladies, not to mention a lot of men, would take it as just that. To me, it's more of a warning that he believes he holds all the cards, and I suspect he uses the same smile if he has to kill up close. As it happens, he does hold all the cards this time. Or the cards that I want anyway. *Go fish, Cassie.*

"Let me guess," he says. "You want me to talk to the Redwood girl, right? Like I said before, darlin', it ain't happening. Business is business, she should know that in her line of work."

I did try to get Devin to smooth things over with Lori. I work with him in a minor capacity on a regular basis, and her—admittedly understandable—hatred of him for killing her brother may make that difficult, at least in my head. Devin had done his research on the things that Lori had turned up during her journalistic excursions, and he'd argued that they've both wrecked lives and both followed their own views of good and bad, they just worked in different ways. He was very firm on that, which made me glad I hadn't told Lori what I was doing. That's not why I'm here today, though. I shake my head and take up residence in the seat opposite Devin.

"No, it's not that. Thinking on it, I doubt that Lori would have been grateful anyway. I was just being stupid and trying to...whatever. I need something else."

"Is that right? Well, in that case, shoot."

"I'm working a missing dog case for a client who wants to remain anonymous. That's going to be a problem, though, because I'm gonna need to slap a few warrants on people for some CCTV footage. No named client means no warrant, and I can't just make something up because the pre-issue checks mean that the PD need to verify the existence of the client on the national citizen databases."

"Of course. They can't have ya taking whatever you want under the guise of a legitimate case now, can they? Now, if it's a client that wants to remain anonymous, I'm gonna guess you're working with that Tech Shift performer, Kitsune."

And with that, what little semblance of a poker face I had drops. Devin laughs, and it has the same arrogant undertone as his smile. "Don't look so shocked, Caz, it ain't hard to figure out. If it's nothing more than a lost pet, then there aren't many reasons that the client is gonna want to remain nameless. Since Kitsune's only travelling through and they make a point of hiding their identity, it was the most logical call. Now, with the right links, you could probably find out who they are easy enough, but I've got no interest in that. As long as his show's good tomorrow afternoon, s'all good with me. What I want to know is why you've come to me?"

I sigh. "If you've figured out who I'm working for, then you know damn well what I need from you."

Devin laughs again, and says, "Yeah, I do that. I just wanna hear you say it." He leans forward and takes another swig of his bourbon. "C'mon, darlin', entertain me."

"Fine. I want to borrow one of your false IDs to use as a client name. An easily verifiable one, not one of those backdoor, underground ones that make you look like an ex-con."

"Huh. Well now, I didn't hear the magic word."

"Oh, come on."

"No please, no ID. Politeness don't cost ya anything, Caz."

I glare at Devin, and he flicks his eyebrows expectantly. I grit my teeth and manage, "Please," and he starts laughing again.

"See? Now, was that so hard?" he asks, downing his remaining drink. "Sure, you can borrow one. I reckon that Mike Frost should be fine for what you're wanting. I'll get the details sent to your normal e-mail in an hour or so. Just don't go getting the poor guy dragged into anything too unsavoury. He's a nice guy."

"Great," I groan.

"Relax, darlin'. I only dick around with ya because I like ya. Believe it or not, unless you do something stupid, you're on my *no-kill* list."

"Good to know," I reply and get to my feet. "As it is, you're on my *don't-be-stupid-enough-to-try-to-arrest* list."

Devin smiles and shakes his head. "Hey, Caz. We ain't friends, you don't get those in my line of work, but you're about as close as you can get with me, so I'll tell ya this one for free. I'm glad you've got a case to work on right now. Do yourself a favour and concentrate on it. Don't take on anything too big for a few days. There're rumblings way down below that things could get real messy for a while. I know that things tend to snowball around you, so try to not to get caught in any avalanches, yeah?"

I raise a curious eyebrow at Devin, but I can see that I won't get anything else out of him. His eyes are stony, and his jawline is too relaxed, which means he's locked that particular door. "Thanks," I say. "I'll see myself out."

MORE COFFEE AND a light dinner in a local takeaway means that I make it back to my apartment a little before eight. Once I get the door open, I am greeted immediately by Bert, whose "caw" of a welcome essentially translates to "Oh, it's you. And what time do you call this?" Judging by the way his eyes are flashing, I can put Bert's apparent grumpiness down to him being low on battery, so I set him to sleep mode and plug him in to charge in the living room.

I noticed that I had both a missed call from Kitsune and a new voice message the moment I left Devin's place, but looking at the time, there was no point calling Kitsune back as they'd probably be doing their final prep work for tonight's show. I could have checked the message there and then but decided against it. If I hadn't been stupid enough to knock my cell onto silent after calling Kitsune earlier, I would have heard when they called and happily discussed things in public. Listening to messages, though? I'll only do that if it's absolutely necessary. When I'm talking, I step almost entirely into work mode. In this case, that would have meant being very careful with my wording so as not to attract the wrong kind of attention. When I'm just listening, I start trying to pick out anyone who may be listening in, which distracts me from the message and leads me to having to repeat the task. Multiple times.

Now that I'm alone, though, I have no qualms with hitting the speed dial for voice mail.

"You have one new message," I grumble, mocking the automated voice that precedes my inbox raid.

"Please confirm next action," the voice says.

"Play message."

"Hi, it's Kitsune, just returning your call. I guess you're busy at the moment. You're right. I know Northfleet Apartments because a charming old lady dumps some water out front every morning and always gives Fish a fuss. I think she leaves the water in the sink overnight to soak some bowls or something, but I guess you don't need to know that. I didn't notice the music store, but I definitely head up by Cross Street to get to the park. We walk right through and out the other end, eat at Cartwright's, then come back the same way. I'd go sightseeing, but I'm not great with directions. Symptom of the work, right? I'm never in any one place long enough to learn the best routes, so I tend to find one route and stick to it both ways. Anyway, sorry, I'm babbling. If you need anything else, let me know." The recording goes silent for a few seconds, bar some light static, then Kitsune adds, "Bye."

"End of message. Please confirm next action."

"Save message to online storage folder Case Retrieval."

"Message saved," the phone replies, and I hang up before it can ask me to confirm any more actions. The way I understand it, voice-activated phone menus used to be awful, especially if you had an accent. Modern tech has improved the functionality, but the menu voices are pretty damn annoying. I wouldn't mind the emotionless tones if it wasn't so obviously a simulated voice. I mean, I get removing the accents and natural vocal quirks makes it easier to understand, but it's so ridiculously cold and tinny. I'd honestly rather they used some bored person under orders to monotone everything in slow, clear sentences. But hey, I'm not exactly the poster girl for embracing all things new and modern. Hell, I even prefer text messages to online messenger services, though that at least is because people tend to hack the messenger streams but don't bother so much with text. The funny thing is texts are technically *less* secure than the messengers these days, but because of that, people avoid sending too much by text and hackers don't bother wasting their time with them. Using that as a reason to use text more makes me feel like I'm getting one up on any potential personal-life-privacy-invaders. I'm using my own paranoia to justify using their beliefs about potential content against them. That makes me smile.

I make a quick coffee and head past the office, or rather the desk reserved for work and sometimes breakfast, that divides my kitchen and living room, and lower myself onto the coach with a groan. Kitsune using the same route there and back means it'll be a bit easier to figure out which cameras to use. I should start deciding so I can figure out how many warrants I'll need... No. This mess with Lori has been eating at me all day. Plus, this case is supposed to allow me some time off, so I think I can justify spending some time trying to fix things with my girlfriend rather than working myself to... *Girlfriend? Have I actually called her that before?*

I shake my head and give Lori a quick call because talking about this over a distance is cowardly but more comfortable. The phone rings once, twice, three times, which is when she normally answers, then rings a fourth and fifth time before a scraping sound cuts in and Lori slurs, "Hi Cassie! How's the case going?"

I laugh without thinking and comment, "You're drunk."

"I am not," Lori replies indignantly. Someone in the background asks something and Lori tells them, "She thinks I'm drunk... I am not! You are... are... Jane thinks I'm drunk. Can you believe that?"

"Really? I don't know what gave her that idea."

"Yeah, see? Cassie doesn't think I'm drunk, and she's a detective, so she can tell these things." I can hear Jane laugh in the background and Lori whispers into the phone, "Ignore her. She just doesn't want to be the only one that's in-ib-ri-at-ed." She pauses then says, "I'm doing it, I'm doing it. I was talking to Jane, and she was saying some stuff, and I was wondering if you're free tomorrow? I kinda need to talk and stuff."

"Yeah, I don't see why not. It'd have to be in the evening though. Is that okay? Maybe seven or eight?"

"The evening. Yes. I'll be here."

"Well, I was only calling to say hi," I lie. "I'll let you get back to your evening. Say hi to Jane for me."

"Cassie says hi," Lori says, her voice slightly muffled. She comes back to normal volume then and says, "Jane says hi too."

"You two have fun."

"We will. G'night, Cassie."

"Good night, Lori," I reply and hang up the phone, a big grin on my face. That's the first time I've spoken to Lori while she's drunk, and I for one am glad to see she's every bit as bad as she said I was on our first date. While I would have preferred to sort this mess out tonight, Lori is in no fit state to talk things through right now, and that in itself is enough of a convenient excuse for me to run away and try to talk another day. Face-to-face *is* a better way to do it anyway, even if it means having to stew on it tomorrow if I fail to suitably distract myself. If neither of us ended up hanging up on the other, I was going to ask her about how the servicing went after the potential argument, but that can wait until tomorrow too. In this state, she'd probably fall into an endless cycle of double entendres.

"Well, I guess I better get back to work."

I hold the power button for my tablet and it powers on with a cheerful, "Good evening, Cassandra." I've got to hand it to Lori, the tech guy that she recommended worked wonders with the thing. It may not be as fast as some of the newer models the shops are trying to push on everyone, but it's working a lot quicker now than it has in a long time. Without the frustrations of a slow-running system to contend with, I've also become more aware, while the audio is still clearly computerised, the developers of this system at least tried to get the machine to imitate some form of vocal emotion. It's *not quite* authentic, but it's a lot better than the phone company manages. I guess the telecommunications companies either have smaller budgets or simply don't care about stuff like that.

I tap the voice command button and the machine asks, "How may I be of assistance?"

"Copy new files from primary folder phone link subfolder Case Retrieval to primary folder case files subfolder Kitsune. Verify when complete."

The tablet flickers once and opens Kitsune's electronic file, showing the audio file has copied successfully. I double tap the file and listen through it again to make sure it's intact, then hold the voice command button again. After the standard question, I say, "Delete all files from primary folder phone link subfolder Case Retrieval. Verify when complete."

The screen flickers again and opens the now empty folder for me.

A bright and cheery jingle from my phone draws my attention, and I'm surprised to see a message flash up confirming that I have a text from Jane. I met Jane while I was working Lori's case and managed to put my foot in it with her pretty quickly. Despite our clashing a little at times, mostly due to a combination of her forward-yet-cheeky personality and my standoffish tendencies, I *do* like her. I open the message and read through it quickly.

Just calling to say hi, my ass. You be gentle with her tomorrow, Cassandra Tam. She knows what she did, and she wants to fix it. She's a screw-up, but she means well. Especially when it comes to you. Remember that.

Okay, so she definitely *does* want to talk about the same thing. Well, doesn't that just ramp up the pressure and take away the flee part of fight and flight? I rub my eyes and send a text back.

I know, and I want to fix things too. You two enjoy yourselves. I mean it.

I put my phone back down on the table, close the folder on the tablet screen, open up a new text file and start noting the key camera locations that I can remember. Nothing quite like work to distract you from your first real fight with a new partner, eh?

Chapter Four

HAVE YOU EVER noticed how the morning seems to just sneak up on you? I swear, one minute I was lying in bed listening to the quiet buzz of Bert's charging dock in the next room, and the next thing I know I'm trying to blink the sleep out of my eyes while I listen to the quiet *clack-clack* of the now fully charged little gargoyle as he patrols the apartment for intruders. For him to be on patrol, something must have spooked him. If it had been film night, I'd say it was me crying in my sleep while my dream self runs away from some horrible monstrosity, but last night was a fairly tame mix of work and a short documentary about the sudden increase in numbers of the aptly named Vancouver Island wolf back home. No, I don't remember any nightmares, and I can't hear any death screams from elsewhere in the apartment, so it was probably just a car outside in the early hours.

I groan as the light of the morning creeping through the Venetian blinds finally penetrates my eyes, and I suddenly become aware of a few things. First, I seem to have managed to slide out from under the bedcovers at some point, and they're now bunched up into a rough tube-like bulge next to me. If they'd been a person, they would currently be dealing with the ever-so-dignified position I've rolled into, which I can best describe as being akin to a face-down drooling starfish. Where work has been so hectic I've not been eating properly lately. I've lost a small amount of my pooch too, which has apparently resulted in my sleep shorts slipping halfway down my butt. All I need now is for the cami top to slip down too and I'd fit right in at the brothel I had to hunt through to find a suspect in a petty theft case two weeks ago.

"Real catch you are, aren't you?" I grumble, pushing myself up into a sitting position.

And there goes one shoulder of the top.

Great.

BREAKFAST, SHOWER, DRESS and head out. It's an easy, well-practised routine that only falters when I have to think seriously about whether to bring Bert with me. Today, it's a simple decision to make. I have a few friends in the PD, and even those I don't know personally are usually helpful in the end, so I have no desire to make it seem as though I want to intimidate them. And as for the CCTV footage? Business owners in that area don't tend to fit into the category of "handle violently," so I see no reason to make my first impression one of malicious intent.

I tell Bert to keep an eye on things and make my way to police station. Upon arrival, I take about three steps through the door and start glancing around for a familiar face, and in doing so, completely miss the short man in front of me. Given the pile of files that go flying, I think it's safe to assume he wasn't looking where he was going either, or he would have stepped around me. Yeah, let's go with that.

"Jeez, Tam," Corporal Devereaux groans, pushing his ill-fitting glasses back up his nose. "What am I, invisible now?"

"Please, Will, I'm like a giant next to you. But hey, it's not the first time that you've missed something obvious, right?" I reply with a wink.

Devereaux smiles and pushes a short *tch* out through his teeth to let me know what he thought of my joke. He had been the original caseworker when the PD investigated Lori's brother's death, and he'd initially viewed my taking the case on as a dig at his own skills. I think he'd said something about me not being the only Canadian investigator around here, and that PIs needed to learn to trust the PD. When I then found that his initial conclusions had been wrong, that was it; I'd earned an enemy for life. Or until Captain Hoover stuck his nose in and set Devereaux straight, anyway. That's experience for you, though. The young corporal hasn't been out of the academy for long, and to have his first major case overturned was a real blow to him. Like Hoover said, or yelled more likely, William Devereaux needed to develop a thicker skin to last out in this job, and that started with *trying* to get along with the city's most respected PI.

I can be nice sometimes, and I liked the sound of *most respected*, so I cut the kid some slack. I still remember how scary New Hopeland can be when you start out, even if you've had some experience already. The way we all balance the quirks of the city is a hard concept to grasp for bright-eyed and bushy-tailed newcomers. Devin sometimes calls the process the *Politics of the Underground*, and it's a good way to think about it. So, we talked, we ranted, and we smoothed things over. Since then, we aren't what you'd call close, but we *are* at least able to joke with each other and not be too obstructive. That being the case, I squat down and help gather the luckily sealed case files.

"Is Hoove about?" I ask.

"Nah, he's at home today. I think his moustache got the flu. You needing something then?" he replies, dropping his guard and letting the thickness of his accent come through.

"Yeah, a couple of blank warrants."

"Well, I can help you with that. Come on." He walks towards his desk. I follow closely behind, and he asks, "So, whaddya working on?"

"Nothing too heavy this time. Missing dog."

Devereaux raises his eyebrows behind his glasses. "Awful lot of *them* lately," he comments and pats the stack of files that we picked up. "About a third of these are missing dogs."

"Huh. Any suspects? Maybe our cases cross over."

Devereaux shakes his head. "None. Even when we've got footage of someone taking the dogs, the culprit's been careful to hide their identity. They certainly know where the cameras are, anyway, and they've got little ball things that fuzz the cameras."

"Little...you mean frag balls?" Devereaux shrugs and I elaborate, "Little silver spheres, about an inch and a half in diameter. They explode and scramble the screen on photo and video equipment."

"Sounds about right. Where'd they come from? Maybe I can get a lead from there?"

"I doubt it. They were kid's toys a few years back. They were top sellers for a couple of months, but the stores were forced to take them off the shelves after some kid chucked them at a friend's face. Kids plus small explosives equals hospital trip, who'd a thunk it? The fuzz only lasted two or three seconds, though, so I doubt they'd be much use here unless you've got Olympic sprinters running the dognappings."

"These balls fuzz the screens for anything from thirty seconds to two minutes, so it sounds like they're something slightly different. They could be new derivatives, though, so that's a starting point. Thanks for that. Some of the dogs are probably runaways too, eh?"

"Probably. I don't think mine is," I say, taking the tablet Devereaux is now offering to me. I start filling out the form boxes on instinct. "Did you want to send me any photos you have for the dogs? If I come across them during my investigation, I can let you know?"

"Sure. If you send me a shot of yours, I'll keep my eye out here too. I don't suppose you caught the wolf documentary last night?"

I smile. "I'm not as obsessed with the Wet Coast as you are, but yeah. It's good to see the population recovering. My grandfather was terrified of them, but I used to love watching them moving in and out of the shadows on a clear night."

"Ah, so you lived near the outskirts?"

"Nah, I think there was just a small pack that was desperate enough to follow the foxes into the urban areas."

"Maybe once things have settled down you could go and take a look, then? Bring back some memories?"

"You trying to get rid of me?"

"Nah." Devereaux laughs. "I think it's a shame that you don't visit the place, is all. Home is home, eh?"

"That's...complicated," I say, and hand back the tablet, forcing as pleasant a smile as I can.

Devereaux shrugs. "I still can't believe how easy it is for PIs to get warrants here."

"There are more of us working in the city than you think, Will. You just won't see most of them because there are only a few of us that have earned the right to easy access. Or in my case, was ballsy enough to just walk in on my first day."

He laughs again. "Well, good luck, Tam. I'll have these processed for you in about five minutes."

I nod my thanks, and we part with a smile. It's nice to have a little piece of Vancouver here in the city, but it hurts too.

WITH MY WARRANTS cleared and ready to go, I make my way back to the theatre and request to speak to whoever would be in charge of releasing security footage for review. The slightly bored teenager working the front desk puts a call out for the building manager and, after a minute or so of waiting, Mr. Patternoster, a man as stern as he is beyond retirement age, greets me with a wary handshake.

"Miss Tam, is it? I understand that you're some sort of investigator. Police, is it?"

"Private, I'm afraid. My father was a cop, though, and I do work with the police when I can."

"I see," he says, making no effort to hide how unimpressed he is. "And what can I do for you today?"

"I was hired by Kitsune," I say, trying to deflect the old man's mood with my best help-me-I'm-nice smile. "They had a dog with them when they arrived at the venue a week or so back, but something happened two days ago, and the dog has gone missing. I'm trying to find out if the dog ran away or if it was taken. That being the case, I was hoping to take a look at your CCTV footage if I could. I have a warrant if you need to see any paperwork."

Mr. Patternoster holds my gaze and sniffs loudly. "Yes, well, any fool with a modicum of tech skills can fake a warrant these days. You'll forgive me if I find this all a bit dubious, Miss Tam. There are plenty of people who would like to see Kitsune without their regalia, and their manager, Mr. Smitt, has tasked me with ensuring nothing is done that would risk this happening. *That* being the case, I am afraid I simply cannot help you. I don't hold with the more prying members of the press at the best of times."

Now, that's a problem. Even if I serve the warrant on him, Mr. Patternoster clearly has no intention of taking me seriously. Ordinarily, my response would involve either a fist, a gun, or Bert. Given that he's just an ordinary guy trying to do his job though, I'd rather not resort to that. *Let's try a different approach.* "Kevin Smitt, eh? Yeah, he got me to sign a waiver when I took the case on."

Mr. Patternoster simply crosses his arms and glares at me with all the patience of an incredibly angry hand grenade with the pin pulled.

"OK, look," I sigh. "You clearly aren't going to listen to anything that *I* say, but maybe you'll listen to Mr. Smitt and Kitsune. Call them, either one, and they'll confirm the situation."

"Fine then," Mr. Patternoster replies and points a bony finger at the young girl behind the reception desk. "If they cannot verify your identity, however, *that one* is going to call the police." He turns to the girl, and asks, "Do you understand?"

The girl counters his glare with a yawn, and I try not to smile at the old man's grumbles about *kids these days*, and *staff respect*. She clearly doesn't want to be here, but she's doing a much better job of dealing with the curmudgeonly building manager than I am. Speaking of whom, he has now pulled his mobile phone up to his ear and is busy grumbling away to some other unfortunate soul. Is it too much to hope it's Kevin? I'd pay to see those two have a grump-off.

Eventually, Mr. Patternoster hangs up and turns to me. And says nothing.

"Now what?" I ask.

"Now, we wait."

After a moment, a tetchy looking Kevin Smitt appears at the end of the hall. *Score one for me.*

"This is the woman, Mr. Smitt. Should I have her escorted out?"

"Hi, Kevin," I say. "Sorry about this."

Kevin sighs and says, "She's fine."

"So, you really did hire a detective? For a missing dog?" Mr. Patternoster growls, turning to unload a full round of angry facials at Kevin. "Perhaps, Mr. Smitt, you may consider telling me if you're going to do something like this? It would save an awful lot of hassle, don't you think?"

Kevin, not one to be outdone, winds up a scowl of his own and fires back with, "Perhaps, Mr. Patternoster, you may consider hiring some night security. *That* would prevent the need for us to incur such expenses, hmm? Just give her what she needs. And don't bother with checking the paperwork, we've had enough delays today thanks to that hydraulic platform of yours. I trust you've followed the correct legal procedures?"

Spotting that the last question was directed at me, I smile sweetly and say, "Of course."

Mr. Patternoster harrumphs loudly. Without even turning to me, he snaps, "This way, if you please," and starts stalking up the hallway.

It doesn't happen often, but I do sometimes wander into the odd conflict like this. The type that gets resolved by other people moaning rather than me hitting something. It makes a nice change when it happens. *Who needs combat sports PPV? This is far more fun.*

WITH THE ENTERTAINMENT portion of the morning done, the actual work slots into place without any need for a caffeine boost. Instead, I can just make my way through the camera files for the day in question. Opening up the synched files on my phone and skimming through what Kitsune's written in the Case Tool, the potential dognapping took place around three in the morning. *Around* is a clear sign I should probably allow for some error with that, so I start the files at two forty-five.

The multi-screen feature on the security system is quite useful here, as antiquated as the concept is, as it allows me to scan all four sides of the building at once. By the time a black van pulls into the screen on camera two, it's already likely the other three cameras will prove useless. The van is plain black, has tinted windows, and no licence plates. It also came in at a sharp angle from the left side of the screen, which means it drove there through a residential area rather than a camera-heavy retail sector. Unless that was just a coincidence, they'll probably leave the same way.

I enlarge the screen for camera two and watch as a man steps out. He's about average height, with little build visible through the loose-fitting black clothing, and no face on display thanks to the old school balaclava. He pulls something out of his pocket, braces himself with one hand on the nearby wall of the building, and throws it towards the camera, causing a mist of static to cloud the screen. *So, he knew where the camera was, exactly like in Devereaux's cases.*

I can still sort of see him through the static, at least enough to know when he walks out of shot and presumably towards the tour bus. Nothing happens for a while, and the snowflakes on the screen seem to have gammed up the audio too, resulting in a layer of hiss that almost entirely masks the single bark of Fish in the background. The fuzz starts to fade, and the man dashes back across the screen to throw what I'm hoping is an *unconscious* Fish over the driver's seat and into the back of the van. He jumps in himself, slams the door shut, and pulls out at speed, turning back the way he came, and effectively blocking me from tracing his movements without checking every camera in the city.

OK, let's see if we can get something useful here.

I roll the video back and step it through the moment after the man got out of the van frame by frame. After a little jumping back and forth between frames, I manage to freeze the video just before whatever he threw at the camera detonated, and zoom in. The item he threw is, unsurprisingly, a small metallic ball. The sheer length of time the static lasted means it definitely wasn't the withdrawn toy. Devereaux may have been right that it could be a derivative, though. If I don't turn up anything myself, I'll have to check with him in a day or two to see if he found anything.

Moving the shot down, I can see the man in the background, bringing his hand up quickly to cover his eyes. Jumping forward a few frames shows a small white glow on his gloves, both on the top of the fingers and open palm on the hand guarding his eyes and on the fingers of the hand he has pressed against the wall.

That seems familiar, I think. I'm pretty sure I saw something similar the last time I visited the city's Mall. It looks kinda alternative, so that narrows it down to one store if I'm right. I pull out my phone and load up the webpage for *The Devil Wears…*, New Hopeland's one attempt at forging a local fashion enterprise for those who like things darker than the big-name designers manage. A quick tap down to the gloves section takes me to the current top sellers: thick black things with steel-look patterning on the top and bottom of the gloves. The description says that they combine design work from two of the most studied subcultures of the early twenty-first century by using a motocross style glove base but a sleek metallic patterning that would have fit in with certain parts of the cybergoth movement.

I sit back and cross my arms behind my head. "Well, there's a crossover. So, I'm looking for someone who looks completely average and owns fashionable gloves. I could warrant the store for receipts, but that would only cover local purchases, not online ones, and there's going to be a *lot* of those."

I sigh, save some screenshots, and make a copy of the relevant section of video. Looks like I'll be relying on someone being too obvious in how they were watching Kitsune on his rounds.

SOME DAYS, THINGS just don't go my way.

Retracing the route that Kitsune had detailed meant my first stop was Northfleet Apartments. There were no visible external cameras and a quick check at the desk confirmed that the only outward facing one is on the door panel at the front of the building. There are plenty of cameras inside, and each and every room has a lock-down setting, so there's no real point in reinforcing the outside, apparently. Meanwhile, the cameras on the various traffic crossings are all road-facing, meaning that they're designed to catch speeding lumps of metal, not regular people, their dogs, and their potential stalkers.

Cross Street stretches on into the distance from there, and most of the stores have their own security measures. As it is, Seventh Son Music, which uses an animated sign on a large video screen to openly describe itself as New Hopeland's number one retailer of music and instruments, is the only one to which Kitsune will have been close enough to offer any potential value. While my client may not have noticed the two-building-wide shop on the corner of the street, its cameras certainly noticed them.

Unfortunately, given the lack of specific details in terms of the description of the suspect, the best I could do with over an hour of video-watching was rule out about three people out of every fifty who were heading the same way.

I already knew the park cameras were dealt with by one of the local government agencies, so I skipped over looking for someone to talk to there and headed straight for Cartwright's. Partway up Dunstone Avenue, I noticed an old client entering one of the houses on the residential side of the street. Given they used a key, it's a safe bet they live there, so that explains why the place seemed familiar. If I get desperate, I'll give them a knock and ask if they saw anything.

The staff at Cartwright's were helpful insofar as they remembered Kitsune. Or rather they remembered Fish and were mortified to hear he'd gone missing. They were more than happy to let me view the necessary footage, which led to several hours of reminding myself that the problem with looking for an average-sized man with little else to go on is almost everyone is average sized these days. Much like with Seventh Son Music, I got to save a bunch more photos of random people, safe in the knowledge it was unlikely any of them were involved at all. Unless the regulars of Cartwright's were even more enamoured with Fish than the staff were, of course. I did get a free blueberry muffin and some sort of hazelnut latte, though, so that was nice, if not overly useful.

The next stop was the Local Government Key Building. While the online goings-on in the city are primarily dealt with by two Governmental Monitoring Offices, the real-world stuff is all based in a non-public-facing high rise that was given the name of a "Key Building" because it's *key to the safe and continued running of the city*. Yes, that's the sort of mindset I have to deal with whenever I head over there and start brandishing warrants. There's also the issue of the staff apparently having to take a course in the art of being higher up the paranoia scale than most PIs. That meant on top of needing to ensure my paperwork was immaculately completed, I also had to put up with a supervisory worker whose job it was to not only ensure I was only checking what I needed to, but to be as annoying as possible so as to make the idea of going there again as uncomfortable as possible. Unfortunately for them, I am well aware that my continued visiting as and when needed in spite of their attempts to put me off is even more annoying for them than their best nuisance-makers are for me. A word to the wise: annoying me then giving me an opening to annoy you more in retaliation is borderline idiotic.

I probably sound a little anti-government there, or at least a bit antagonistic. What can I say? Having a senior official kill your father can do that to a girl. And besides, when the staff are helpful, like they are at the Governmental Monitoring Offices, I'm more than happy to play nice. Inhibitive suits with nothing better to do than make my job more difficult? They can deal with my wrath. And I have so many different forms of wrath that I can pull out, depending on my target.

Long story short, another couple of hours wasted switching between watching some incredibly boring footage and confirming that yes, I am only checking time periods likely to be relevant to the case, revealed some less than startling results. I did learn that there *are* a few well-hidden cameras facing the open fields, but neither these nor the nature trails revealed any potential suspects on first viewing. I'm also pretty sure that the customary checks of my saved data took longer than they needed to. I guess my temporary shadow didn't have any other unfortunates lined up to torment and just wanted to make sure that he did as thorough a job of winding me up as possible.

After that, I headed back home and set myself up on the table that comprises my office. I shot a quick message off to Lori apologising that I was going to be a little late and promising to make it to hers around nine, give or take. Then I started running through a number of checks I knew would be far easier here than at the various locations I'd visited. First, I set my tablet to copy the files and rig together some single video files covering each journey to and from Cartwright's. Even with time signatures, that wouldn't be too easy if I hadn't given the saved copies of each individual location a standard naming convention. The machine may be old, but it can handle piecing together files titled *Day 1 A, B, C* and so on in order.

With the computer working on that with the copied files, I moved onto the originals and loaded a few up at once in a panelled view similar to the shots at the theatre. While this did show that one or two men did indeed follow the same route as Kitsune, none of them fit the size of the van driver.

I was left with four possible conclusions. One, the van driver was working alone and either already knew about Fish or had spotted him at a different time, and so didn't need to do any trailing. Two, the van driver was assisted by someone else, but only so far as them spotting the dog and noting where he came from. Three, anyone doing the reconnaissance was as well acquainted with the camera positions in the area as the van driver was with those at the theatre and so knew to stay out of the way. And four, several people were assisting the dognapper, and so almost everyone in the photos and videos is a legitimate potential suspect.

By half eight, the glamorous life of a PI on a missing pet case with little to go on and too much material to be useful had gotten to me and I decided to call it quits for the evening and head on over to Lori's. One cab ride later, and I was ready for some conversation that didn't involve one-sided ranting about the state of paid transport licensing since the new officials had been nominated and voted in. Sorry, Mr. Transporter, but I have my own job-related nonsense to deal with, so my sympathy well has run dry for the evening.

In the end, I made it to Lori's just before nine.

I GIVE THE doorbell a quick press and take a step back to admire the serene feeling exuding from Lori's bungalow. Hell, Foster Street as a whole is like that; all the new-build homes here are decked out in the old-world trappings of a typical all-too-perfect suburban hideaway. From my limited experience with the neighbours, it's a nice, peaceful area that's well suited to the older generation looking to settle down. It's an odd way to think about it because at twenty-four, Lori is three years my junior, and *I'm* not exactly nearing retirement age. Still, she likes it here, so good for her.

Lori opens the door, decked out in a baggy green and black striped jumper, a pair of black boot cut jeans, and a fluffy pair of slippers in the shape of alligators that open and shut their mouths as you walk. I can't help but smile at that, and Lori returns my smile, albeit a bit more nervously than normal. I guess we're both well aware how this could go.

We hug, and Lori leads me in by the hand. "Beer?"

"Sure," I reply, slouching into what has become my normal spot on her two-seater couch. "I'm off duty for the evening now, so I don't see what harm a drink will do."

"Off duty? You could'a fooled me." Lori waves a can of something imported up and down at my work clothes.

"Hey." I wrap my voice in mock offence while I take the can. "I came straight here after a long shift. I was gonna change, but figured why delay the visit even more? Sorry about that, by the way. I've spent most of my day going through CCTV footage and trying to reconcile the different shots and angles to find...anything, really."

Lori sits down next to me and sips from her own can. "Any luck?"

"Right now, I may as well declare about seventy percent of the city a potential suspect." I take note of Lori's slightly closed body language. I've learned pretty quickly that the easiest way to get something out of Lori is to not dance around the subject too much. If she's aggressively stubborn, finding out what's wrong becomes a trade-off of "this ails me, what ails you?" When she's like this, a gentle but direct approach works wonders. Unfortunately, that's not so easy for me right now. "So."

"So."

The silence hangs for a moment until I decide to take a deep breath and try to kick things into motion. "OK, look. I think I know what you want to talk about. What happened in Kitsune's changing room was..." I shake my head and put my beer down on the floor, then lean back into a stern, cross-armed pose. "There's a reason I waited until last night to call you. I'm angry, Lori. I'm *really* angry, and it's a struggle not to start shouting at you right now. If I wasn't convinced that, on some level, you honestly believe you were in the right, then I wouldn't even be trying to hold back. *Diu*, I hate how that makes me sound. I mean shouting, obviously."

"If it'll make you feel better, you *can* shout."

"Don't tempt me."

Lori's nostrils and mouth twitch a little at the flat statement, making her look like an adorable but concerned bunny rabbit. I think better of mentioning that and wait for her to take a bigger gulp of liquid courage and say, "I think that I may owe you an apology."

"May?" I say, making the word a question drowning in disbelief.

"No, do. I *do* owe you an apology. It's just that... Okay, so you know how Jane said I've not always had the best of luck with partners?"

"That's not how she put it exactly, but yeah."

"Well, when we were talking last night, I mentioned what happened after the show and how you seemed sort of off with me when we left, and...she kinda said something that made me think I may be panicking a bit and trying to...maybe...be a little more controlling than I need to be."

Lori catches my raised eyebrow and her eyes widen a little as she blurts, "I'm not making excuses. I just want you to understand why I acted the way I did. I mean, when people have screwed me over before, it's kinda felt like I've left myself open to it by being pretty hands-off. Like how you haven't said that you have a problem with me getting drunk with Jane every now and then. That doesn't bother you, does it?" I shake my head and she continues, "I was like that with partners too, but I should have probably been a little more worried. That's not the build-up to a confession or anything, and I'm glad you trust me, but...when I've been trying to look after you, I think that part of it has been a way to subconsciously keep an eye on you."

I frown then, and repeat, slowly, "Keep an eye on me?"

Lori nods. "I do trust you, Cassie. I've trusted everyone that I've ever dated, 'cause that's important, right? But I think that part of me is on guard a bit. And I know that's wrong, I do. It's not like I've been secretly sneaking around after you and keeping tabs on where you are and who you're with or anything, I've just kinda become focused on making sure that you're okay and that you're not struggling or anything like that. It's stupid, but I still blame myself a little for how people have treated me before. I mean, not in every case, some people are just...but some. Some were my fault, I think. Like, Ink. When Tanya left me because she couldn't handle Ink being a part of me, that was *my* fault, because I couldn't back down about it. So, with you, I think I'm sort of trying to create a constant reminder of how much easier I can make things for you, almost as a compensation for the bad stuff. Does that make sense?"

Argh. Now I'm beginning to think that this is as much my fault as anyone's. Okay, Cassie, deep breath. Deal with Ink, *then see what else needs to come out.*

"No wonder you were getting drunk." I sigh. "Look, Lori, at no point should *anyone* view Ink as bad. Given the role she has in your life, I'd say that she's about as far removed from bad as you can get. Sure, I'm not *entirely* comfortable around her yet, but that's because this is all new to me. You know about some of the stuff I saw when Tech Shifting first hit the streets, but the cases I told you about weren't even the worst ones."

"Wait. They weren't?"

I shake my head. "Do you remember the last major one that hit the news? Uh, the guy used to smear messages on the walls? I was still working with the PD on the cases then. I had to help investigate the crime scenes, Lori. When they were fresh. When they still stunk. When they were still *wet*. That sort of case leaves a lot behind when you're done with it. In a way, I guess I was never really done with it. So, when I started dating you, it was a culture shock for me. Even now, I still have to make an effort to push certain images back when you're in TS mode. *But*, I make that effort because I *never* want Ink to come between us." I sigh ruefully and add, "Maybe I don't make that clear enough."

"No, no, no," Lori stutters. "This isn't you. You haven't done anything to make me think you'd do anything like that, it's more like a...a subconscious preventative measure, I guess? It sucks, whatever it is."

"No. I get it. I'm not exactly free of hang-ups myself."

"But *mine* are spilling into *your* work life now. When I yelled in to Kitsune that you'd take the case, that left you without a choice on it, didn't it?"

"Yeah. Yeah, it did."

Lori's head drops, and I catch sight of the first tear as it falls onto the couch. After a quiet sniff, she says, in a small voice, "I'm sorry."

I'm not heartless, not when it comes to people that I actually care about. If I still had an appetite for self-destruction like before I met Lori, I'd keep pushing. I'd poke and prod this one until it got infected and slowly ate away at me. I still don't really know what I have with Lori, but I do know I don't want to throw it away that easily. So, I cup my hand behind her head and pull her into my chest, gently stroking the area around one of her plugs while my other arm wraps her in as gentle and reassuring a hug as I can manage. "I meant what I said. I'm not free of hang-ups either. I make stupid decisions. I screw up. To a degree, I *need* someone looking after me and trying to make things easier for me, so it's not like you were heading in the wrong direction with this. You just...drove off the road a bit."

"I'm sorry," she whispers again, and I feel her hand tighten on my side.

"Let's make a deal. If you see me doing something stupid, like overanalysing a flyer for a stage show, tell me and I'll do my best to listen. But don't do it in front of a potential client, and don't try to make decisions for me. Nudge, don't shove. Deal?"

Lori sniffles a *mm-hmm*, and nods against my chest.

"You're good for me, Lori. Don't ever think otherwise."

"Try saying that again when we've been together a bit longer. Six months is about as long as most people last with me."

"Then we'll aim for seven, how about that?"

Lori lets out a small giggle and I look down, meeting her relief-filled, icy blue eyes. She pushes back, coming up onto her hands, and tilts her head up to mine, pausing only to make sure that I'm not going to pull away. Slowly, I lean in to meet her, letting our lips come together in a gentle caress before parting to allow our tongues to meet. I taste the warmth of Lori's breath in my mouth, and let out an involuntary moan, surprising me enough to stall. Lori, realising I've frozen up, gently closes her lips and tilts her head forward, letting her forehead rest on mine. We both smile, and the moment passes. I shouldn't be this nervous, I know that. Lori has been helping break some old habits and walls that I should have dealt with a long time ago, though she probably doesn't know that. Some walls are stronger than others, though, and they're enough to stop me moving beyond a kiss just yet. *It's a good job that Lori wants to take things slowly too.*

"Wanna see some photos from the Kitsune show?"

I pull back a little and ask, "When did you take photos?"

"While you were too absorbed in the show to pay attention to me." Lori giggles, playfully booping my nose. She stands up and walks over to the shelves at the far end of the room to grab her tablet. "It's weird, though. A couple of them came out a bit funny."

"Funny? How so?"

She sits back down next to me and loads up the image set. "Yeah. Like here, this shot's fine, right? Well, apart from that guy getting up and moving seats in the middle of the picture. But if I go to the next one it's all fuzzy and distorted, see? It's the same with the next couple I took, then...they clear up again here, right as the same guy from before gets up and leaves. The rest are all good, though, if you wanna look?"

"I can tell you why the photos fuzzed," I say, smiling confidently and swiping back to the first shot of the guy walking in front of the camera. The man is small in size, with a fashionably neat swept-back style to his hair, but he has the tired eyes of someone who's spent far too many nights without sleep. "What do you notice about what he's wearing?"

Lori looks over the photo and says, "Not a lot. It's weird that he's wearing gloves, though. I mean, it wasn't cold that night or anything. Definitely not inside."

"Exactly. It's hard to see on this one because the chair blocks it. If you look at the second photo of him where his arm is swinging up a bit...there. Can you see those markings on the gloves?" I ask, pointing to some metallic detailing on the thick black leather. Lori nods and I ask, "Have you ever heard of Tappers?"

"I've heard the term," Lori replies, her tone showing that she's thinking it through.

"The story goes that there was a firm working on a covert communication system they wanted to pitch to the military. The idea was that you had two gloves, a tapper and a reader. You hook the tapper up to a computer via cable and transfer in whatever you want to pass on, then take the gloves to where you want to leave the message. It doesn't matter if it's a wall, a pen, a chair, or whatever, you just give it a double tap with the index and middle fingers on the tapper, and the glove will leave behind this ridiculously small digital imprint. When someone wants to retrieve a message, they walk up to where they think it is and give a single tap, but leave the fingers held against the item. If there's a message within a metre radius, the glove will draw it in like a magnet. The reader gloves are used to either select the message to imprint or to read the one that's retrieved. They have a small screen on either the palm or the top of the glove, depending on the set.

"The Underground got wind of it, though, and bought the licensing. What made it such a bold move on their part was that they did it all legally with some ironclad contracts that prevented further development of the system for anyone but themselves and ensured that *no* law enforcement agencies could ever get hold of or use the things. In fact, because of the strict terms of the contracts, if a police officer were to use one to try to track a criminal, for example, they would be facing up to ten years."

"Really?"

"Yeah. Crazy, isn't it? Anyway, were you using your phone for the photos?" Lori nods. "I thought so. The *tapping* emits a small pulse, so that would have interfered with anything close by that wasn't a sturdy enough system. Most high-end tablets and above should be fine from a distance, but below that would be prone. I don't know for sure why the tapping doesn't knock out the reader glove, but I'd guess that the internals are in some sort of protective casing. It's kinda like in some of the security footage I was watching today, though. Fish was definitely dognapped, you can see most of it happening on the theatre security cameras. The guy that did it threw a small scrambling device at the camera and fuzzed it up. Same concept, but intentional...wait..." I close my eyes, an idea forming. The moment it emerges into full view, I slap my own head and laugh. "I am such an idiot."

"What?"

"The guy who took Fish. He was wearing gloves. The way the metal on them caught the security lights, I thought they were from that new crossover fashion range in *The Devil Wears*.... But they weren't, were they? They were Tapper gloves. I haven't seen them for so long that it didn't occur to me. The scrambling ball was misdirection so that he could *tap* the wall and get the security code to Kitsune's tour bus! Could I take a copy of the shots of the guy from the show?"

"Sure. I was gonna say take any you want anyway."

I can see that Lori is a little disappointed, but I'm not sure why. I mean, this is a good breakthrough. I could take the photo to the police station and run a match to see if there's a link and... *Diu. I* am *such an idiot.*

"You know what? That can wait until later. I'm off the clock, right? How about we grab another drink and see if we can find something spooky on the TV?"

Lori's smile returns, bringing with it a reignited playful glint. "Spooky, huh? In that case, should I grab a pillow for you to hide behind, or are you just gonna hide in my chest again?"

I blush at the memory of leaping involuntarily into Lori's protective bosom the last time we watched a film together and shake my finger at her. I'd offer a verbal retort, but I appear to be all out, so I choose instead to beat a hasty retreat to the kitchen.

It's gonna be a good evening.

Chapter Five

THERE ARE FOUR people in New Hopeland who are all but untouchable: Brett Stantz, Gory Gutierrez, Saul Solomon, and Kerry White. Together, they're known as "The Four Kings," and despite all residing within New Hopeland, you're not likely to meet any of them unless things get *really* bad for you. Even then, the stories say you'll be faced with a video screen of a masked person using a voice changer, and the only people that you'll physically *meet* will be paid cronies. If you're lucky, they won't be the last people you meet.

The Kings run the underworld, not just here, but across all of Utah State. When Tapping became a thing, it was the Kings who negotiated the contracts and set about distributing the hardware to the various smaller groups in the cities they hold. They took note of the actions carried out by the different factions, then put a ban on the gloves being used without their direct consent. Getting permission is supposedly only a fraction easier than getting a meeting in the first place, which makes me wonder what's going on with the two sudden Tapper appearances. One thing's for sure, though, if this is something legitimately authorised by the Kings, I may have to back down. If that happens, I'm not taking any money from Kitsune.

With Hoove still tucked up in bed at home, and no doubt grumbling his way through a bowl of hot soup, I made a point of asking for Corporal Devereaux at the station. He was able to confirm there hadn't been any advancements at his end on the mountain of missing dog cases he'd been landed with. I explained what I'd found, and he set the computer running facial recognition on the photos from the show. Like I said to him, the chances are that he'd turn up the Tapper connection eventually too, but with the sheer number of similar cases he'd been given, wading through them was going to be hard going. That's the good thing with only working one case; you get to give it the gold star treatment rather than following the get-this-off-my-desk protocol.

The computer scan turned up a match for a man named Scott Young. According to the file, he has an on-off love affair with the cells here, mostly due to minor felonies. The main thing I needed was an identity for his boss, though, because they would have been the one who needed to get permission from the Kings. When Allen Fuerza's name popped up, I took my leave and grabbed Bert.

ALLEN FUERZA IS a dangerous man, not because he's a particularly badass gangster, but because he *thinks* he is. He's easy enough to find because his base of operations outside the virtual world is above a run-down warehouse near the Governmental Monitoring Offices. What makes it laughable is that he specifically chose to set up on the top floor of the shabby old building as a way of demonstrating that he's *above* the underworld. Were he actually as competent as he liked to claim, the Kings would have taken care of him a long time ago. As it is, he's more likely their equivalent of a humorous satirical comic strip.

Still, the problem with people who are dangerous in that way is that they'll act up like they *think* the genuine big shots do. If I turned up unannounced somewhere to try to get a meeting with someone like Brett Stantz, I'd be an idiot, but I likely wouldn't get more than a little roughed up. With Fuerza, I'd be looking at a full-blown execution. Or attempted execution followed by a lot of explaining to the police, anyway. So, I rang ahead using a number that I'd gained in a case a few years ago and let him know that we needed to talk.

Ever the gentleman, he sent some goons in cheap suits to greet me at the door and do their best to intimidate me with a laughable mix of posturing and a clear show of their semi-automatic Berettas. I simply smiled, petted the little metal monstrosity on my shoulder, and let them lead me right to their boss. And so, here I am, waiting patiently for a self-important moron to stop looking me up and down like he runs the city. I also notice that, while he has a luxury chair to sit in, I get to stand in the middle of the room. He does enjoy lording his status over his guests. Finally, he waves to his goons and says, "It's fine. We're old acquaintances in a way, aren't we, Miss Tam?"

Weird wording, but we have met before during a few cases, I suppose. I shrug. "Sure, why not?"

Fuerza smiles and tells the goons, "Send the Palomas in. They may as well get to know our friend here."

The three apes leave and, a moment later, two new men replace them. One is an angry young man who's complimented his suit with a tangle of long ginger hair held in place by a beer-stained bandana. The other is strangely calm and hiding behind a pair of expensive-looking sunglasses which, when combined with his neatly shaven head, gives him the appearance of a typical TV hitman. They walk through the room in silence and take their positions either side of Fuerza, standing tall with their hands crossed neatly in front of them.

"Don't you already have a Paloma in jail?" I ask.

"Yes, well, after his little escapade at your place, he has found himself demoted." Fuerza nods to Bert and adds, "I believe your friend there saved me the bother of demoting the other one."

"*The other one*? Do you forget their names when they become *brothers*?"

Fuerza smiles and rests his chin on his knuckles. "Of course not. Unless you have reason to ask, though, their names aren't important. You know how this city works, Detective. Branding is the key to success, is it not?"

I roll my eyes because now that I'm in front of him, Fuerza is more likely to feign respect for me *not* pretending to be afraid of him. Hell, he knows as well as anyone that the Paloma Brothers are a joke. He can try to build them up as a pair of top quality hitmen who will work cheap as much as he wants, but there aren't many people out there who don't know how bad they are, let alone how rare it is for the Paloma Brothers to actually be related.

"I admire your moxie," he says, right on cue. "But I'm a busy man. I understand you have a photograph to show me?"

I nod and step forward, reaching into my pocket. Out of the corner of my eye, I notice that Sunglasses Paloma has tilted his head subtly to follow my movements. It's such a small movement that you wouldn't notice it if you didn't know what to look for. Looks like Fuerza lucked out and hired someone who actually knows what they're doing this time. *Best behave yourself, Cassie,* I tell myself, and pull out the print I took of the two pictures from the Kitsune show.

"Scott Young. He's one of yours, right?"

"He is."

"Do you notice what he's wearing?"

Fuerza lifts the sheet of paper closer and frowns, which tells me that he does. As if to further confirm this, he clicks his fingers towards Sunglasses and beckons him to look at the photo. The brief glance they share gives me the opportunity to get nosy and flick my eyes over the small table next to Fuerza's *throne*. Unfortunately, there's nothing of any real interest: a small stack of what appear to be annotated and highlighted bank statements are piled haphazardly on top of a thick hardback book, *Four Steps to Power* by Casille di Franco. It's a political thriller, if memory serves. I only read it the once, at Charlie's recommendation. As books go, it's fine, though outside my normal genres. From what I can see of the cover, the text is printed backwards on this copy. There's a bubble-wrap envelope underneath the book, but I have no way of telling what, if anything, is inside. For all I know, it could be what the book was delivered in. *Ah well. I guess a pre-signed confession was too much to ask, even for Allen Fuerza.*

"I'm working a case right now and the only suspect I have was wearing Tapper Gloves. I *don't* think that it was Mr. Young, but I'm sure you can see why I'd come to you with this. Given the look on your face, I'm guessing you didn't know that Mr. Young was going Tapping?"

Fuerza's lips twitch and he narrows his eyes at the pictures. "Admittedly, I did not."

"Have you given permission to *any* of your people to go Tapping recently?"

Fuerza glances at me and asks, "Do you have a warrant, Miss Tam?"

I cancelled the unused warrants from the CCTV run because I'm a good little detective. They wouldn't have held enough sway for this anyway. "For this specifically? No. I can get one easy enough, though."

"No need," Fuerza says, waving his hand dismissively. "If I'm not under warrant, then I can talk frankly without having to consider whether what I say can be used against me by the police. May I have your word that what we discuss will not be used in such a way?"

I shake my head and smile. "You know I can't promise that. If you're the one pulling the strings in my case, then I'll have no choice in how I use the information you give me."

"I see. Tell me, Detective, what sort of case are you working on?"

I stand in silence for a moment, thinking through my response. If this were something on a bigger scale, I wouldn't mention the specifics to Allen Fuerza or anyone else in the Underground unless I had to, but all things considered, I can't see that it will hurt. "Missing dog."

Fuerza blinks, then, being the arrogant idiot that he is, bursts out laughing. "You came all this way to talk about Tapping, and you're investigating someone's missing pet?"

"The person who took the dog was wearing Tapping Gloves," I reiterate, and fix him with a stony glare. "Given the pictures of Mr. Young, it's not a big leap of the imagination to assume that *your* organisation is involved. Given the ban on using the equipment without permission from the Kings, I'd hate to think that you're trying to run some scam under the radar."

That stops Fuerza's laughter dead in its tracks, and he lets out an angry sniff. "First of all, Detective, I don't run *scams*. Second, even if I did, what use would I have for some random dog?"

"You tell me. There are a lot of missing dogs out there right now, Mr. Fuerza."

New Hopeland's number one wannabe crime lord taps his fingers irritably on the armrest of his chair. "No, I have not authorised any Tapping. Nor would I be so stupid as to do so without the Kings' permission."

"Then perhaps you could tell me where to find Mr. Young?"

"No, I don't think that I can."

"Fine," I reply and turn to leave. "I'll be back with a warrant."

"Miss Tam," he says, and I stop in my tracks, but don't turn around. "Please understand my position here. Mr. Young's actions hold the potential to have an adverse effect on me personally, and from what you have alluded to, there may be more within my organisation who are carrying out similar work. *I* will deal with this. Once I have spoken to those involved, I will either give you the information I have gathered, or I will hand over Mr. Young, in one piece and perfectly capable of being questioned. Does that seem fair?"

I nod but keep facing the door, because that lets him know I view myself as holding all the cards here. "Sounds good to me."

"Good. I'll be in touch within the next couple of hours."

ONCE I WAS home, figuring I could be in for a long wait, I made a start on tidying the "currently working" drawer in my bedroom filing cabinet. The term "currently working" has always been applied in a very loose sense with the items in there, as it's rare for me to have too many cases on the go at once that would require any physical space, yet the drawer always remains packed out. I decided that, in keeping with the traditions of the drawer, I would also take a very loose approach to the term "cleaning." While the vast majority of items therein could have been destroyed there and then, if not scanned and disposed of, it would feel too unfamiliar to have it empty. Instead, I set about putting the contents into some sort of order. Well, I used elastic bands to gather things from individual cases into single piles and chucked them back in in no particular order. Maybe when I finish the Kitsune case, I'll get rid of one of the piles and replace it with the photos and prints I have scattered on the desk. *Scattered, huh? I should probably band them up too before Bert decides to shred them like he did with the unsorted bill pile.*

True to his word, Fuerza gets in touch three hours after our meeting. That surprises me because, given his normal ineptitude, even a rapid check of his Tapping gear should have taken him all day to sort out. I agree to make my way down to Cartwright's to collect the information, hoping desperately that he hasn't done a rush job on this. Inaccurate information is worse than no information, after all; when your clue store is barren, you keep looking everywhere, but when it's full of the wrong stuff, you look specifically in the wrong place.

The staff of Cartwright's remember me from my previous visit and I find myself spending some time deflecting questions about the case while they make me "another of those hazelnut things," as I called it. In the end, I take the simple approach and tell them that I am following a lead and someone is going to meet up with me to provide some information that may help get Fish back. Wanting to avoid any unnecessary problems, I tell them very truthfully that I'm going to be meeting some nasty people and that if we're interrupted, it may cause issues both for me and for them. I apologise for bringing such a situation to their place of business, but they're very understanding. Allen Fuerza may be on the bottom rung of the criminal ladder, but that's still a lot more dangerous than these folks are. *It does make me wonder why he selected this place in particular, though.*

I take up my position at the table situated to the left of the main window, exactly as Fuerza had requested. That's odd too, his insisting on a specific table. *With his sudden increased speed, should I be worried about him taking out a hit on me or something? Nah, that's just my old friend paranoia paying a visit.*

I'm busy thanking the waitress for my second latte when Sunglasses Paloma turns up carrying a thick leather bag. He nods to me when he enters the cafe and heads to the main counter. When he sits down opposite me, he has a cup of tea with him, with the bag still in the cup and a small metal pot of milk next to it on the saucer. "Personally, I prefer to pour the milk in before the hot water," he says, carefully adding said milk to the drink and giving the cup a gentle stir with the small teaspoon already sticking out of the cup. "I find it far easier to judge the amount that way."

His movements are, much like they were back at Fuerza's place, subtle and deliberate. I look him over. He appears to be in pretty good shape, with his muscular frame barely hidden beneath the suit. A thin scar peeks out from under the left side of his sunglasses, slightly discolouring the otherwise darkened tone of his skin. He takes the spoon out of the cup, dumps the teabag into the empty milk pot, and places the spoon gently down on the saucer before lifting the cup and taking a sip. It's all very precise. If I didn't know better, I'd have thought he was ex-military, possibly even high ranking, at least on the action-facing end. But that would be crazy.

"I'm surprised that you guys got things together so quickly," I say, getting my concern out in the open.

"Understandable, given Mr. Fuerza's reputation," he says, his deep voice neutral. "I can assure you, though, that *I* am perfectly capable of inspiring efficient working practices, regardless of the underlying quality of the staff."

"I'm getting that impression. But if you're that good, why work for Fuerza?"

His response comes in the form of another silent sip from his cup.

Well, that's a clear "you're not getting any significant information out of me." I raise my own mug to my mouth, less carefully than Sunglasses, and take a gulp, but keep my eyes on him as closely as I'm assuming he did with me from behind the darkened glass. "So, what did you find out?"

"That Mr. Young did indeed use a Tapping Glove at the central theatre, precisely when you said he did. There have also been several other incidents of this happening. Including Mr. Young, the number totals around twenty of Mr. Fuerza's staff, though there may be one or two others, and one or two of them may have been doing things on their own and the unauthorised use of Tapping Gloves is coincidental on their part."

"Jeez...that's a lot to go through. So, is that's what's in the bag? The details of all of them?"

"No. You won't be getting the details of those who have been Tapping without Mr. Fuerza's knowledge."

"I see," I reply and raise my cup to my mouth. I don't take a mouthful this time. The movement is a distraction to avoid him seeing my free hand start to slide to the edge of the table and down to my pocket.

"I wouldn't," he says, and I stop still, a bead of sweat suddenly forming on my forehead. "I spotted your Familiar Unit on the roof when I came in. I can assure you of two things right now, Miss Tam. The first is that, should you try to summon it, I will kill you before it reaches you. The second is that, if you choose to behave in a rational manner, you will soon see there is no need to summon the machine. You are assuming that my not supplying the details of the Tappers means I am here to cause you harm, but that is not the case. I will be providing you with something far more useful."

"OK, I'll bite." I lower my cup. "I should warn you, though, if I call Bert, he *will* kill you, even if you get me first."

Sunglasses nods and takes another mouthful of tea. "There are things in motion that are of a direct detriment to Mr. Fuerza. He may be among the least respected of the underworld, but he is not without his secrets, Miss Tam. Tell me, how many people do you think it takes to learn a secret before it can become dangerous?"

"Depends on the secret. Sometimes one person, sometimes many. If it's the right sort of secret, no one knowing can be just as bad."

"In this case, one person who was not authorised to know certain things made a discovery on his own. The reason I am not giving you the information that you, logically, expected, is that they are acting in the manner they are because this particular individual is blackmailing them on the basis that they have been carrying out side deals without Mr. Fuerza's blessing. Mr. Fuerza was already aware of this fact, but the deals were of no consequence to him, and so he did nothing. These individuals were not aware of this, however, and so the threat of him finding out was enough to cause them to carry out the orders of another. They were undoubtedly responsible for the recent rise in dognappings in the city, but that is, I hope you will agree, unimportant."

"The puppet master is more important in the grand scheme of things, that's what you're saying, right?" Sunglasses nods and I continue, "In terms of the overall end game, you're right. For me personally, not so much. My job is to find my client's dog. Given that you've obviously found out a lot more than you're saying, can you at least tell me whether I'm likely to get the dog back alive?"

"I believe so, yes. The information we have obtained has been through covert scanning by a small team of trusted individuals. As it stands, neither Mr. Fuerza nor myself have moved against those who are being blackmailed, though the time will come for us to do so. That in itself should ensure the safety of the missing dogs, certainly for the time being."

"Because if you move too soon, they may panic and do something stupid, eh?"

"At which point, you would no doubt contact the police yourself, leading to a full investigation of Mr. Fuerza and his operations in relation to the matter. If we work together, however, we can ensure that not only do you achieve *your* goal, but that we achieve ours."

"And what *is* your goal, exactly?"

"That, Miss Tam, is simple. The actions of the individual responsible for this situation constitute a direct challenge to Mr. Fuerza, and in particular, one of his more lucrative operations. Our aim is to resolve said conflict in a manner that is of benefit to Mr. Fuerza."

I don't like this. It's too sensible for Fuerza. For now, I'll have to play along, though.

"Okay, so what happens now?"

Sunglasses pulls an envelope out of the bag and pushes it my way. "Open this later. It contains the details of the *puppet master* as you called him. This includes known locations where he is likely to hide, should that be required. If your primary aim is to recover the stolen dog, however, I recommend you do not use this information to track him down just yet."

"Then what do I do with it?"

"You hold it in case things do not pan out in a preferential manner. Our recommendation is that you use the next piece of information you acquire to build a case for some police assistance. I hasten to add, though, Miss Tam, that what I am about to give you in addition to this is being provided only if you give your word that you will not personally target anyone but the person named within the envelope unless absolutely necessary. Though they have strayed, the puppets may yet prove to be salvageable assets. You would also be expected to ensure that, should you acquire their assistance as advised, the police are aware that Mr. Fuerza claims no responsibility for the actions of his staff in this instance."

I narrow my eyes. "What am I walking into here?"

"Something unpleasant. Do we have your word?"

I sigh. "Fine. Unless provoked or threatened, I will focus on whoever is in this envelope. And if I contact the PD, I'll be sure to tell them what a good boy Allen Fuerza is being. Good enough?"

"Indeed," Sunglasses replies, and he stands up. "You are aware of course that the deal The Four Kings forged legally prevents me from supplying you with Tapping Gloves, or even telling you what I could learn from using one. In fact, I am myself legally required to take steps to ensure that the information I acquire from using such items is not given directly to any law enforcement agency or individual connected with one."

"Yeah. And?"

Sunglasses doesn't respond. He simply walks to the counter and asks to borrow a pen, then returns to our table. He opens the leather bag, pulls out a pair of Tapper Gloves, and slips them on. Once they power up, he taps the fingertips of the reading gloves under the table and says, "The pulse interferes with small electronic devices, so taking a photograph of the details on the display panel is impossible. It is a necessary security measure, but it provides some challenges." He looks down at the small screen on the reader glove and makes a note of the details on a napkin. Once he's sure that he's copied it correctly, he removes the gloves, places them neatly in the bag, pulls his phone out, and takes a photo of the napkin. "Once the charge dies down, you can, of course, do what would have been more convenient to begin with if it didn't open up the possibility of any item with a decent zoom being able to photograph the screen. If you were wondering, my own phone has been modified with a protective case to avoid the effects of the gloves, though that in itself required special permission from the Kings. Now, all that remains is to dispose of the manual copy." He walks towards the door, tossing the napkin in the litter bin before he leaves.

I blink, walk calmly over to the bin, and remove the neatly folded piece of tissue, scanning the words carefully.

ONE DOGFIGHT TO END FUERZA'S REIGN. ATTENDANCE IS MANDATORY. GLOVES WILL BE SUPPLIED AT EVERY CHECKPOINT. USE AND THEN REPLACE. FIRST CHECKPOINT IS AT THE ENTRANCE TO THE WEST SEWERS. ESTIMATED WALK TIME IS TWENTY TO THIRTY MINUTES. FIGHT BEGINS AT 17:00.

No date means this is a temporary message, set for today only. Whoever's named in that envelope is trying to take Fuerza down for who knows what reason, and he's trying to do it by running a damn dogfight.

"*Diu,*" I growl, screwing the napkin up in my hand.

I'm shaking with anger. Rather than storm out of the building and risk making a dumb decision, I decide to stick around and try to calm down a little first. If nothing else, Bert will no doubt be enjoying the buzz of scanning the area for signs of dangerous activity. It may not be the busiest street in New Hopeland, but the flow of people is at least constant enough that there will be plenty for him or keep an eye on, which will hopefully shake off some of the frustration he's been feeling. *Frustration? Is that even the right word? I'm not even sure how far along the accepted AI scale he is.* I shake my head. *That thing's like the Kinsey Scale for neuroscientists and robotics engineers. Way above my head.*

I sigh. There's nothing quite like reminding yourself that you're a long way from understanding how the things around you work to bring you back to reality. I feel a gentle hand on my shoulder and turn to see the waitress standing there with a worried look on her face. "Is everything OK?"

"I hope so," I reply, mentally kicking myself for scowling at an innocent. "Is there any chance I could get another cup of the same?"

"Of course," she replies, her smile returning. "The gentleman in the suit insisted on paying for your drink too, even though I told him you'd already paid, so technically, we owe you one."

I blink. That was unexpected. "Oh. Well, thanks to him, then."

"I'll have it with you soon. You just sit down and have yourself a break. It's good to chill out once in a while, right?"

"Yeah. Yeah, it is," I concede and walk back to the table. I slide into the seat and pick up the envelope that Sunglasses gave me. It isn't overly packed out, but with the way he's held himself, I expect that's more to do with only giving me what I need, rather than not being thorough enough. There is definitely something unnerving about the guy. He's got a similar feel to Devin if you're ever unfortunate enough to encounter him at work. He doesn't come across like an assassin, though, more someone who *could* be an assassin if he really wanted to. There wasn't a hint of any doubt in his voice when he told me that he could kill me before Bert could bust in too, and that makes me believe him all the more because it's amazing what a bit of confidence can push you to achieve.

My drink arrives nice and quickly, and I peel the envelope open and pull out a small wad of papers held together by a paper clip. Flicking through the pages, it reminds me a lot of the reports that the police hand out when they're planning to take down a Mr. Big, better known, to me at least, as the Canadian Technique. The idea is to set up a fake criminal organisation, seduce the suspect into joining, and gain their trust enough that they confess to whatever crime it is you're trying to pin on them. To get things moving, a good deal of time is spent on surveillance, learning as much as you can about the suspect so that you can play into their habits. Judging by what's in front of me, someone within Fuerza's group is adept at knowing what his *staff* get up to. If I didn't have a job to do, I'd spend some time questioning whether this was a new improvement for the man himself, or whether he was never as ridiculously inept as he seems to begin with. Actually, no, if I didn't have a job to do, I wouldn't have these papers in front of me at all. Not that it matters. The only thing I can be sure of is that Fuerza is not himself part of a Mr. Big.

According to the file, the ringleader of this little escapade is named Malcolm Castleford. He's a plain looking middle-aged man with prematurely greying hair and a thick moustache that not only puts Hoove's to shame but adds a few years to his appearance. The photo is similar to what you'd find on most ID cards but, even without seeing anything below the upper chest, I can tell this isn't the man who carried out Fish's dognapping, at least not directly. His shoulders are a little too thick with the beginnings of excess weight for him to fit the average look of the man because "average" around here means in a little better shape than this guy appears. Though that doesn't matter either. If he's pulling the strings, then it's him I need to get anyway.

The initial profile shows that Mr. Castleford holds a couple of accountancy qualifications, though not as many as the major players. That would be why he's also listed as acting as Fuerza's Financial Executive, a role that the brackets after the title show as encompassing accountancy, general money management, staff finances, and investments. By this, I mean that people with fewer qualifications tend to either be content with their position or just starting out. Being in his late forties, Castleford seems too old to be starting out, though I'm not ruling out him being a slow mover. The firms who insist on their staff having more letters and acknowledging bodies after their names are at the top of the game and will absolutely *not* take on anything clearly dodgy because, since the IRS crackdowns of the late twenty-second century, they've *all* been under close scrutiny as a matter of course.

Given his age and mid-level list of certifications, my guess is that Castleford *wanted* to make it to the big time but missed the boat for whatever reason. That would mean he has enough ambition to want to make some big money but is smart enough to know that his chances to do so are limited at this point. Accountancy is a young man's game, or so they say. If you're in that position and are willing to get your hands dirty, then moving money for a crime lord can give you a good opening. In addition, at least seventy per cent of your own work would be perfectly legit, and it would only be the money you had to physically get involved in gathering that would have the potential to land you in hot water. But hey, even then, some trouble with the law would only prevent you returning to the straight and narrow. If anything, it would give you a badge of honour to wear for the Underground stuff.

Of course, with ambition comes risk for the employer if you're a man like Allen Fuerza. The Tapping message was clear in stating the aim of tonight's *entertainment*, and I use that term with all the disdain it deserves in this case, is to bring Fuerza down. There's no confirmation in any of the paperwork as to why he wants this outcome or what exactly he hopes to achieve, though that doesn't surprise me. Right now, I'm damn near working as a troubleshooter for the lowest branch of the crime tree, though Fuerza knows that's only out of necessity on my part.

Sunglasses has given me a pretty comprehensive list of Castleford's regular movements and haunts, and assuming he isn't just *really* good at blagging things, he could have taken Castleford out at any time. And that worries me, since what it means is that there's more going on here. I doubt they're worried there's something in place to ensure the plan goes off regardless of whether or not Castleford is caught, as having me deal with it wouldn't change that. No, Fuerza has a reason to keep Castleford alive. What was it Sunglasses said? Their aim is to resolve said conflict in a manner that is of benefit to Mr. Fuerza? They must think Castleford can still be useful in some way. That's the only thing that makes sense.

Let's see what he has on the people he's blackmailing. The ones whose definite involvement they were able to confirm all had similar things going on; financial deals with people outside the organisation. That wouldn't normally be a problem. Plenty of criminals have their fingers in a lot of legitimate pies, even the small-time perps Fuerza surrounds himself with. In this case, though, the deals are with people known to be involved in organised crime outside of Fuerza's control. The notes say Fuerza was already aware of them thanks to his own *watchdogs*, as well as Mr. Castleford himself.

That must mean Castleford has been keeping himself in Fuerza's good books so he can take him by surprise.

As additional information, the notes say that the deals are with two types of people. The first are people already a short way above Fuerza in the chain of command, which he doesn't object to because they probably aren't going to move on him. The second are all new transplants to the Underground, both from outside and inside New Hopeland. The key here is that they aren't a threat, and so a little collusion isn't going to harm his own business.

Good old overconfidence, I tell myself, then frown.

I drum my fingers on the table and stare a hole through Castleford's photograph. *Am I overthinking this? Even if Sunglasses isn't faking his efficiency, and even if Fuerza is exaggerating his stupidity, he really isn't the sharpest knife in the Underground's armoury, I'm certain of that. What was it that Devin said? There's rumblings down below? Somehow, I can't help but feel like I'm being used here. That leaves two questions; who's doing the using, and if I want to find out, how loud do I have to shout to avoid causing an avalanche but still attract the yeti I'm interested in hunting?*

"First things first," I grumble. "I get Fish back. After that, maybe I'll know whether to keep poking this one or try to back off."

Try to back off? That's different. Smart too. Lori would be proud.

Chapter Six

THE ENTRANCE TO the Western sewer tunnels is technically just within the bounds of the city, though most prefer not to think of them as such. The fact is, humans like to think of things as being nicer than they are. Even those in the know about how New Hopeland operates are stuck with that need to view the world around them as pleasant. So, some people choose to disregard the tunnel entrance due to the smell. Others don't like the look of it, either because the general aesthetic sets them off or, in the case of those who stick to the modernised areas of the city and avoid the retro-focused spots, because it's too old-fashioned for their tastes. Then, there are those who can't quite bring themselves to dislike it for such silly reasons, and they instead choose to place the blame on the fact that the area is often used as a pick-up point for illicit goods. Of course, minor laws make it more likely that someone from outside the city will be dealt with to the full extent of the main laws, so those who live here and wish to collect such goods usually have to walk fifteen feet away from the tunnel entrance in order to pick them up. Why? Because, like I said, the entrance is technically still within the city limits, regardless of how many citizens say it's not.

Thankfully, the entrance is also in an area with plenty of convenient things for me to hide behind. I am well aware that I don't know exactly where the Tapping Gloves are hidden, and as far as I can tell, around twenty people are going to be coming here looking for them. Yeah, they're low-end Fuerza goons, so they aren't exactly going to be appearing on any most wanted bulletins, but twenty idiots versus one idiot with a Familiar still weighs in the favour of the larger group, even if I do have the PD monitoring my location. Speaking of which...

"Another three just went in," I say, keeping my voice low and my finger pressed to the transmit button on my earpiece. "That makes twelve in total. Are there any other visitors heading this way?"

I release the button and the earpiece crackles a little before a voice responds, "Two more cars are pulling in and heading your way. You're lucky that it's such a quiet area. If this had been Main Street, we'd have never been able to tell who was or wasn't heading in until they were almost on top of you."

I smile. That's Lieutenant Hanson for you. When it comes down to it, she's the no-nonsense, take no prisoners type, but when the action hasn't yet started, she's chatty, even if it means having to point out the obvious to her. "Yeah, well, I doubt it's going to be quiet too much longer. If it's clear after this group, I'm gonna have to head in after them."

"You sure you don't want to wait until all twenty are accounted for?"

I *had* considered that but decided against it. "Negative. If I use the Gloves myself, you've gotta arrest me. I'd have rather followed the smaller group, but if this lot are on the way, it makes the risk that they'll catch up to me too great, especially if the other group moves slowly. I'd rather know that there'll be the option to hide and pick up where I left off if I lose the targets."

"*Negative?*" she snorts. "Somebody's all professional today."

"I'm always professional. Couldn't you tell?"

"Two months ago, Tourniquet. You, a Tech Shift chick who I happen to recognise as one of your clients, and a whole lotta alcohol. You were *real* professional then, weren't you?" I freeze and feel a blush rising. When I don't reply, Hanson laughs and says, "Don't worry, the others are out having a smoke, so it's just me talking to you. I've wanted to catch you with that one for *so* long, but you're always surrounded by people at the station, and I wouldn't want to embarrass you in front of those clowns."

"How did you...? You were there?"

"Guilty. I would've come over to say hi, but you looked like you were having a great time, so I figured I'd leave you to it."

"I...I can't believe you..."

"Sure you can." She laughs again. "C'mon, Cassie, we've known each other since you started working down this way. If you'd known I was there, then you would absolutely have known I was gonna ride you for it. You may not have a badge or an academy certificate, but you're one of us. That makes you fair game. Besides, I don't play with just anyone, only the really cool people, so it's kind of a badge of honour for you."

"Gee thanks. Why bring it up now, when I'm about to head into a potential snake pit?"

"A couple of reasons. It's the first opportunity I've had, and I don't know when another one's gonna come along. Then there's the tenseness in your voice. I figured that you were a little nervous and this would lighten the mood a bit. Plus, when a colleague's feeling like that, it's good to remind them that we've got their back, even if we don't always outright say it."

The two cars drive by the sewer entrance and park next to the four that arrived before them. Four people get out of the first one and three get out of the second, then both groups converge to talk nervously among themselves. That leaves at least one more person to come, so my safeguard is still in place. That's good. "Ya know, you're right. I think you were the first person on the force to have to deal with me, weren't you?"

"Probably, yeah."

"And in all that time, I've had one thing I wanted to ask you and never did. Mind if I ask now?"

"Shoot."

"What *is* your first name, Lieutenant Hanson?"

She laughs and dodges the question with another. "How many are there?"

"Seven. It looks like they're about to go in, so unless there's another car heading this way, I better get down there."

Hanson pauses then says, "No, you're clear. Give us the signal when you need us to bust in, and I'll let you know if anyone else turns up. Oh, and if the Tapping kills the earpiece, don't worry too much. It's set up to reset itself automatically. Good luck, Cassie."

I nod, realise that the good Lieutenant won't see my response, and decide not to answer verbally out of embarrassment. Instead, I pat Bert and say, "First priority is to disarm and subdue, do you understand?"

"Caw."

"I mean it, Bert. No maiming, unless absolutely necessary."

"Caw."

And with that, I creep out from behind the mass of rocks that have been hiding me and slide my way down the hill. The smell hits me at about twenty feet from the entrance. It's vile. It's also an annoying distraction because I'm going to find that really hard to block out. That's a problem because I'm relying solely on my own eyes and ears here. Well, more my ears, because it's near pitch-black inside. I'd have let Bert do the tracking, but there are disadvantages to that. If he's scanning for movement in an area of low light, his eyes take on a very bright, very red glow, which is also very, very obvious. His movements during the process are also about as quiet as the finale to most firework displays. That's not entirely his fault. When you're made of metal and have a generally boisterous attitude, noise is a given. It'd be fine if we were trying to scare the people we're tracking, but no, this one requires subterfuge.

With Bert sitting silently on my shoulder and his eyes in a low power setting so as to avoid being seen, I make my way in, walking slowly and listening as intently as I can. The—I'm gonna say water because I don't want to think about what else it might be—is running, adding to the ambient noise. The walkway is a little slippery too, which will make moving quickly difficult if I need to do so. On the plus side, the same things will apply to the group ahead. On top of their nervous chatter, the running liquid will help mask my own movements, and the lack of a decent footing on the floor should mean they don't get too far ahead of me. They also seem to be heavier footed than me, which gives me another sound to latch on to. The tunnels aren't entirely without lighting either, but what's there is poorly maintained and doesn't serve much purpose other than to offer a faint glow at the edges of the stone walkways and gently bobbing *items* in the slop. It means I'm also stuck having to keep one hand on the damp wall. *Damp? More like cold and sticky.*

I'm not picking up on too much of the actual content of what's being said up ahead. Other than the occasional loud outburst, the group is keeping things quiet, which makes me wonder where these tunnels are running under. They're probably worried about being caught. My hand finds a turning on the wall and someone starts to grumble about something not being worth it for a few extra bucks on the side. The voice is low, but close, which means that they've stopped. I slip back behind the turn and wait. A static fuzz fills my earpiece for a moment. *They must be Tapping.*

I wait for the fuzz to die down and for the footsteps to resume, then I wait a little longer so that I'm not walking too close behind them. From what little I can make out, the group seems too preoccupied with their disdain for Castleford's methods to actually notice me, but it wouldn't pay to get overconfident and drop the careful approach just yet. We walk in a straight line for another ten minutes or so, until I hear the faint sound of boots on metal. Frowning, I push on and find another turning, but there are no sounds coming from down in the darkness. I sigh and make an instinctual decision. *If there's no sound coming from the shadows, they must have kept going.*

I walk on and find myself irrationally happy to see a metal walkway bridging the flow. That explains the metal clunking at least. Interestingly, I can see from here that the sewer is set out identically on both sides of the running waste. Each side tunnel, barely visible with the poor lighting, is matched by another on the opposite side. I must have missed that because I was too busy paying attention to the targets. Speaking of which…

Taking care not to fill the area with the same echoed steps that I'd heard, I walk across the bridge, taking note of the light buzz that creeps into my ear. *More Tapping. It's weak, though. It must be further on this time. I'll have to speed up.*

Moving as quickly as I can without both safety and sound becoming an issue, I soon come to another turning. I pause long enough to check there are no signs of movement, then move on, trying to find *something* to catch on to. Just as I'm about to double back and check down the last tunnel, a loud scraping noise cuts through all the other subtle constants. I keep moving and, the moment I find myself at another turning, the noise comes again, but louder.

I turn and make my way down into the darkness, noting that the wall has changed from cold and sticky to warm and less sticky. Small mercies and all that. Partway down, I find a small power generator pushed up against the wall. And I mean small. From the feel of it, it's about the size of Lori's temperature maintaining box.

That makes me smile, and my mind drifts back to the night she convinced me to go to the Kitsune show, essentially kick-starting my involvement with this mess. *That was a good cup of coffee. What did the instructions say? If you put something that isn't already prepared, it gets confused and overheats? That's like me right now. She sent me into this case unprepared, and now I don't have a clue what I'm doing down here and feel like just setting Bert loose to track these idiots down. Ugh. Work time, Cassie.*

I shake my head and try to focus on the task at hand. The generator is resting on what feels like a metal table. It's warm too, which means that it's running, probably to power the lights. Having stopped already, I wait and listen. At first, nothing but the ongoing ambience filters through, but then, a loud fuzz cuts into the earpiece again.

That's closer than the first one. I should be able to hear them.

But there's nothing else.

I pat the generator gently and realise that it's not doing what I thought it was. I haven't come across any others along the way, which would mean that, unless the others were either hidden or off down the tunnels I skipped, it's been powering a large area of lighting. Even as bad as the lights are, there's no way this thing is supplying all of them. When I feel it, the cabling is sticking out to the side too. Why wouldn't you have it pushed up so that the cables were behind it? And none of this explains the scraping sound.

Crouching down, I let my hand follow one of the table legs down to the ground, then use a single finger to explore a small hole. It runs back towards the cables. I feel around, and quickly confirm that there are identical pits extending under each leg. *Guiding tracks?*

With no sounds coming in to guide me, I decide that I may as well work to that assumption, and move to the side of the generator with no cables sticking out. I give it a shove, which is pretty difficult with an immobile Familiar on your shoulder, regardless of how lightweight he is. The table scrapes noisily along the wall until it reaches the end of the holes. A quiet *click* sounds, followed by an equally quiet *swish* at my feet, bringing with it some proper light. I crouch again and see that the light is coming from a small crawlspace. Well, it's the height of a crawlspace and it's built like a crawlspace, but the general shape is closer to that of a vent from some science fiction movie. Whichever way I look at it, it's got to be where my targets went, which means it's also where I've got to go. Which creates a new problem.

I lift Bert from my shoulder and place him in front of me on the floor, then whisper, "Bert. We're going inside, but I need you to be as quiet as possible. Do not give verbal responses unless you need to warn me of something. If you understand, flash your left eye."

A red light flashes in front of my right eye and I open my mouth to start chastising the shiny little menace, then realise that he was flashing *his* left eye, not the eye in front of my left. So technically, he did what I said. "OK, you first."

Bert clacks forward into the small area, and switches to a slow waddle, minimising some of the noise. I follow after and, once we get a couple of feet inside, the opening behind us swishes closed again and the sound of grinding metal fades in behind it. The crawlspace doesn't go on too far, and we soon find ourselves nearing a well-lit opening. It sounds quiet, so I tell Bert, "Keep going."

Bert obeys, and we come out into a warm, carpeted hallway with some proper lights hanging down from a ceiling high enough for me to stand up and put Bert back onto my shoulder. The hallway seems to stretch on in both directions, and a few feet to the side, there's a wooden door. At this point, there's no way to tell if the group continued on in one direction or the other, or if they went through the door. *The door* will *be the easiest and quickest thing to check.*

Moving quietly, I grab the doorknob and give a tentative twist. It moves easily, and the door begins to slide open. That's a good sign that the group I've been following *may* have come through here. I push the door open enough to slide around and make my way into a darkened room with a distinctly musty smell. The door makes no move to swing shut behind me, and I don't move to close it myself. If needed, it'll provide a good escape route. Plus, the light from the hallway is helping me make out some shapes. The way things are strewn about haphazardly makes the room look like a cellar of some sort. There's a box labelled "clothes" near the door, and next to that an open box of old external hard drives. Around the other side of the door, I find the battered remains of a vaguely familiar looking table.

Somewhere inside Bert, his gears start to turn, and their grinding creates the illusion of a low, mechanical growl in my ear. Then, three things happen at once. I feel Bert's talons tense as he readies to pounce. I hear the sound of a hammer being pulled back and clicking into place in an old-style revolver. And I realise where we are. "Bert! Stand down!"

I turn just in time to see the silhouette of a woman in front of a flight of concrete stairs at the back of the room drop her gun into one hand and whack a light switch, instantly flooding the room with an unnecessarily bright flash of white.

"Caz? What the Hell were you doing in the supply halls?" Charlie asks.

"TAPPERS," CHARLIE SAYS, incredulously. "In the supply halls."

I haven't told Charlie everything. Honestly, I don't have the time right now, and I'm a little preoccupied with trying to get a response from my friends on the currently poorly named response team. She does know that I was trailing a group for a case at least. "Hanson, you there?" I say, my finger held tight on the transmit button, but my earpiece continues to remain silent. I shake my head in frustration. "Yeah. So, what *are* the supply halls?"

Charlie shrugs. "That's no secret. You know how we normally keep stimulants in one place and just pick up what we need? Well, if we're expecting a big order, then we ship them below ground to the relevant Elite. Makes it easier that way."

"So, these hallways connect the different houses for the Elite Dealers?"

"And the main supply stores, yeah. I'm surprised you didn't know about them. When you never asked how I got stocked up for major deals, I assumed someone had told you."

"I thought you just picked them up."

"Huh," Charlie replies, leaning back against the wall and crossing her arms. "I suppose you weren't ever here during a delivery."

I open my mouth to respond, but a voice cuts in on my earpiece. "Cassie, you there?" Hanson asks.

"Yeah, I'm here," I reply, my relief mixing with my frustration. "What happened?"

"We got hit with a bunch of fuzz when they used the first set of Gloves in the tunnels, but the auto-reset didn't kick in. I think you were probably too close and they did a number on the equipment. We lost your tracker too."

"*Diu.* Is it back on now?"

"Yeah. It says you're around Fenchurch Street. That seem about right?"

"Really? You think I'd be able to tell that down in the tunnels?"

"I don't know. Can you?"

"Not down there, no. But yes, I'm on Fenchurch Street."

"So, you're not down in the tunnels now?"

"No, I lost the group and ended up back topside. Any ideas what to do now?"

"Yeah, get yourself back down there. Another guy went in about ten minutes after you. If you're lucky, you'll be able to catch him and pick up the trail again."

I rub my forehead and ask, "And if I get too close to him when he uses the Gloves? Then what? The tracker's gonna cut out again."

Hanson pauses, then says, "It'll come back again eventually."

"Yeah, by which time, I could've been jumped by twenty people with no sign of backup in sight."

Hanson clicks her tongue over the earpiece. That I can hear it means that she's intentionally transmitting it. *Thanks for that, Hanson.*

"You could shout, *really* loud," she tries.

Charlie taps my shoulder and hands me a sheet of paper that reads, *Did the Tapping affect Bert?* I reread it and glance at the little mechanical gargoyle who's wandering around the room and examining the furniture in his ongoing quest for a decent scratch post. "Thank you," I say to Charlie, then hit the transmit button and say, "The Tapping didn't seem to effect Bert. Familiars are built not to be damaged by small surges, right?"

"You tell me," Hanson replies, slightly bemused.

"Yeah, it was something about avoiding the risk of having their programming scrambled too easily. If I send you his tracer details, you should be able to connect to that if the main tracer cuts."

"OK, but what if the comms go down again?"

"If comms go down but you can still follow one of the tracers, then send a team in *if* we stay in one place for more than a minute. If you can't catch either tracer, then send a team to the point where it went down. If the message was right about timings, I can't be too far from the meeting point now. If you can, though, get them to enter from above. The way this is going, the sewers are a direct route to wherever they're holding the dogs, but the actual building will be on street level."

"Roger that. I'll get them ready to move. Keep us updated if you can."

"Will do," I reply and turn back to Charlie, who is now staring at me with a suspicious look on her face.

"Dogs?" she asks.

"Long story. Bert, come here a minute." Bert waddles over and I slide a panel on his stomach aside so I can check the identification number on the outside of his frontal servicing hatch. I hit the transmit button and read it off to Hanson, then confirm that we'll move when we know the straggler has gone by. Bert, being Bert, wanders off completely unfazed. Charlie, on the other hand, is still looking at me. "What?"

"I need to know what our halls are being used for."

I could argue with her on that point, but that would only slow me down right now, so I take the quick route instead and confirm, "Someone's set up a dogfight. The audience is definitely using them to get to the venue. I don't know if they were used to transport the dogs themselves, but it's possible."

"You've gotta be...and when were you gonna tell me that?"

I shrug. "After we stop it."

"Caz, we work hard to not get on the wrong side of the law any more than necessary. Something like that in one of our non-public areas could be *really* detrimental to that relationship. You get that, right?"

Honestly? I hadn't thought about that. In my defence, I didn't know about the tunnels before today, and I *have* been very wrapped up in figuring out how to stop the thing from happening. "The PD know who the group belongs to, and they definitely aren't Dealers. Besides, we're all only after one guy. They'd never pin it all on you guys."

"Except they'll want to ask questions about why the halls were potentially being used to transport dogs, won't they?" I can't argue that one, so I don't. When I remain silent, Charlie says, "I need a name, Caz, so that I can try to sort things out at our end."

"Fine," I sigh. "But leave it to us to deal with him, yeah? His name's Malcolm Castleford. He's..."

"The accountant? Oh, Hell."

A ball of fuzz runs through my earpiece and I squint. Ahead of me, the clock on Charlie's wall glitches, just like it did before the Kitsune show. I nod towards it and say, "I think a Tapper just entered the halls."

We make our way back down into Charlie's cellar and she says, "This could get really messy, Caz."

"It's already messy, Charlie. There's a lot going on here, and the worst part is, I don't know what half of it is."

"No, I mean it could get...okay, not messy, but complicated. Castleford does a lot of work for a lot of people, and if he's going around setting up dogfights, then he's going to be looking at repercussions from more people than he probably realises. We don't do animal cruelty."

"I know."

"*We're* gonna need to talk about this too. Damage control is gonna be a bitch, so I need to know what you know."

I crack the door open and step out into the hall. I can hear footsteps moving off to my left. They aren't running, but they aren't slow either. I pat my shoulder, and Bert starts scaling my leg and making his way up my back. "Look, I promise I'll come and tell you what I can when it's all over. Right now, though, I need to try to stop the fight from happening."

Charlie sighs. "Twenty people, huh? You gonna be okay?"

I pat Bert's head and say, "I'll be fine. I don't intend to actually move in until backup gets there anyway."

"I could give you a million and one examples of when you've said that and done the complete opposite." She groans and adds, "But you don't break promises, so I'm holding you to that talk, even if you have to deliver it from a hospital bed. You better get going before you lose the guy."

I nod and start moving briskly down the hall. There are no dark shadows to hide in here, which makes it lucky there are so many turns and side paths to stick by instead. That's not to say it's a maze like the sewers, it's more that the halls are a bit twisty. They must be built to follow the shape of the buildings above. Maybe they weave in between cellars. I turn another corner and see that the hallway now stretches on a fair distance. Well, far enough that I should be able to see the guy anyway. But I can't. *He must have sped up without me noticing.*

I start to run, barely noticing a gap in the wall as I pass, and end up having to double back a few steps. Studying the offending section, I can see that it's been built from wooden slats, each wallpapered to match the surrounding area. That's weird. One of the boards is loose too, and there's sound coming through from behind it. I close my eyes and listen. *Barking. He must have been in a hurry and not put the board back properly.*

I slide a few of the boards out, taking extra care not to make any unnecessary noise, and slip inside. Behind the wall, I find a dusty, concrete floor, and a scattering of equally dusty crates. There's a set of metal steps off to the side, and looking up, I can see people lining the platform above, staring intently at a space somewhere ahead of me. Most of them clearly aren't happy to be here. I creep around the side of one of the crates and follow their line of sight. We're in an old warehouse. I can tell it's disused because half the windows are cracked, and the lighting is a temporary set of spotlights hooked up to a portable generator. In the middle of the room, someone has set up a circle of smaller crates with tall metal fencing resting on the inside of the circle like a cage. Behind that, a makeshift stage has been set up, upon which stands Malcolm Castleford with a microphone in hand. There's a camera on a tripod next to him, with the lens angled down into the circle. He's talking nervously about how the event is a reward from the boss for all their hard work. Any other time, I would have believed him. *And so would countless others, which is what he's obviously banking on.*

"Hanson," I whisper. "I found the place. It's some sort of abandoned warehouse, I think. How close are you?"

"Not far. We started moving towards you after the last call. Give us maybe…ten minutes, if the traffic stays clear."

"Try to be quicker if you can. This isn't looking good."

Hanson pauses, then says, "We'll do our best. Stay safe."

On the stage, Castleford says, "Without further ado, let's get our first combatants out here."

Someone pulls part of the circle open and I creep to the side to peer through a gap between two larger crates near what's obviously intended to be the entrance to the makeshift arena. I keep my fingers crossed that the opening act is gonna be humans, but no such luck. The first dog being walked into the circle of boxes is a nervous-looking Doberman. Behind that, and being dragged, is Fish. I swallow hard and dart quietly back to my original vantage point, just in time to hear the boxes being slid into place.

The two dogs start to make noise, with Fish whining pitifully and the Doberman barking and yapping. From the way the sound is moving, I'm guessing that the Doberman's barking is aimed at the people up above rather than the other hound. Castleford shakes his head and says, "Looks like these two aren't up to fighting today. But that's okay. Mr. Fuerza gave me some clear instructions as to how to get them in the mood to entertain." I see him lift a large stick up and angle it down in front of the camera. He starts to try to jab at the dogs, and that's more than I can handle.

I climb up onto the crate in front of me and yell, "My name is Cassandra Tam, and I am a licenced investigator of New Hopeland. You are..."

And all Hell breaks loose.

Castleford seems surprised but not overly disappointed. He does drop the stick at least. Everyone else in the room is panicking. There's a lot of screaming and shouting, and a couple of people are making a dash for the doors. Then, a loud *bang* sounds and a bullet hits the crate, inches from my feet.

Bert reacts instantly, soaring up towards the balcony and straight at a man with what appears to be a high calibre pistol aimed towards me. I dive off the crate, barely avoiding the second shot that comes my way, and draw my own Glock. Looking up, I can see that Bert has clamped onto the guy's wrist and is busy snapping at the fingers still wrapped around the gun. I take aim and squeeze the trigger, catching him in the shoulder. He drops backwards and releases the gun, probably not realising I just saved his hand.

The sound of crates being pushed apart draws my attention, and I turn to see two thugs scrambling through the gap and heading straight towards me. From the pained cries up above, Bert has spotted another gunman too. To my surprise, swinging the Glock towards the closest of the advancing foes doesn't scare him into stopping, and allows him to get a grip on my wrist. He twists it, and the gun drops noisily to the floor. I respond by slamming a foot into the side of the guy's knee. It's not pretty, but it's effective enough to make him let go and allow me time to swing a right hook at the other guy who's now closed in, stumbling him back.

The first guy gets back to his feet just as "generic gangster lady with more tattoos than brain cells" sneaks up behind me and grabs my arms. I lash out my foot again, catching the first guy in the jaw, and struggle my way free of the woman's untrained grip a split-second before the second guy swings a punch, causing him to catch *her* around the face. She swears loudly at him, and I make a grab for the Glock, but a bullet slams against the floor right in front of it. A loud scream follows, and a beat-up Beretta pistol clatters to the floor. I go for the gun again, but this time, one of the two guys barrels into me, slamming me down onto my back. I can hear some scraping behind me, and my attacker looks up. His eyes go wide, and he scrambles off me.

I roll over and rise to my feet, realizing immediately why the guy ran. Castleford has finished pushing one of the fenced boxes aside, letting what I'm assuming is every single dog he has back there loose into my little area. My three attackers have escaped back over the crates and shoved them together. They obviously forgot I climbed in to begin with. That said, with a mass of very scared dogs running around, some of which are now staring at me with a fair bit of aggression in their eyes, making a run for it may not be the best idea. The last thing I need is to trigger some long-buried genetic predator-prey reflex.

One of the dogs, which unfortunately for me is a large wolf-like thing, makes a dive at me, and I barely manage to step out of its way. If it had been a human attacking me, I'd have met aggression with aggression, but that is *not* an option right now. These are not criminals looking for a fight, these are scared animals that had no choice about being here.

Some of the dogs have started trying to scramble over the crates themselves now, but the big dog is still trying to get a clear run at me. It darts to the side and growls. In a flash, Bert lands heavily on the floor between us, letting out a loud warning, "Caw."

"Bert, stand down," I command, but Bert doesn't move. He just keeps tracking the big dog and letting out his own growls in response to the animal's threats.

The main doors, hidden somewhere at the back of the warehouse, screech open, and a small team of cops flood in, rifles and voices raised, which sends the dogs into even more of a panic. So much so that, the moment one of the cops shoves a crate aside, it's enough to send them all flooding out into the main warehouse and, from the surprised shouts of my would-be saviours, into the street. Momentarily distracted from his battle of dominance with Bert, the big dog's ears prick up at the sound of its furry comrades escaping, and it quickly joins them in the dash for freedom, knocking the nearest cop over as it goes.

"We've still got one in here," someone yells, and I turn to see them moving slowly towards a crate at the far end of the room. I snatch the Glock and run, hoping like crazy that it's Castleford.

But it isn't.

Huddled in the corner, whimpering sadly, is a mid-sized American Shepherd whose snow-white fur is looking dirty and more than a little ruffled. While I don't recognise the cop who yelled, I do recognise his aggressive stance as he steps forward with his rifle trained on the poor dog. I step closer and place a hand on his chest, stopping him in place. "Lower the gun, idiot," I say, keeping my voice low.

Despite looking slightly annoyed about my choice of words, he does so, and replies, "It's *your* funeral."

I roll my eyes at him, making sure he sees me doing so, and start to move slowly towards Fish. As I get closer, I drop to my knees, putting myself at the same height as the dog, and say, in a soothing voice, "Hey Fish. I'm gonna take you home, all right?"

Fish whines and half-heartedly bares his teeth, giving a few snaps. Somewhere behind me I hear the *clack-clack* of an advancing Familiar and turn sharply, pointing a finger at Bert to tell him to wait. This time, he obeys. When I turn back to Fish, though, he's pushing himself as tight to the wall as he can, obviously spooked by my quick movement. "It's okay Fish, it's okay."

Fish whines again and I close my eyes, trying to think of a way to calm him down. American Shepherds lack the courage and even temper of their German counterparts, and so are rarely natural working dogs. They can bite out of fear, and they *can* get aggressive if threatened, but I already know that Fish is far more nervous than violent. Even without my pre-case briefing, his reaction to the fight scenario proved that. He also has an unusually—for the sometimes loyalty-inhibited breed at least—strong bond with Kitsune, which means he is likely now worried about returning to his master. Thinking back to the contract, that may be my best shot here. *Okay, let's chance it.*

I slide myself closer until I'm within clear biting range of the scared pooch and whisper Kitsune's real name to him. Fish stops whining and looks at me with the scared eyes of a child. I whisper the name again, and he stares at me. "Home?" I say, making the word a question, and Fish drops his head and walks nervously towards me. I reach my hand out and give him a gentle rub on the head. He seems wary, but he's at least decided to take a chance on me.

"Your client's?" Hanson asks, dropping down next to me, and sliding her protective headgear off.

"Yeah. If you don't mind, I'm gonna get him back home before I come clear up the paperwork."

"And if I do mind?"

"Then I'm doing it anyway."

"Glad to hear it," she replies with a smile, carefully running her fingers through her short, choppy black hair, and repositioning it into a designer scruff. "Come on, I'll drop you off wherever you need to go. These guys can deal with cleanup until I return." She glances up at the guy behind me and asks, "Right?"

"Sure," he grumbles and starts walking towards one of his fellow officers.

Chapter Seven

I'VE SEEN KIDS picked up out on the streets for everything from loitering to legitimately being suspected missing. One thing they all share in common is that being escorted home in a police car holds a certain novelty for them. They could be scared or hurt but being able to sit in a squad car excites them. I don't know if it's a symbol of safety, something they don't expect to have to ride in again, or just a learned behaviour from television and books, but it happens more often than it doesn't. It turns out the same cannot be said for dogs, or at the very least not for Fish. I don't know what exactly was done to him in the time that Castleford had him, and I don't know if he was kept purely in the warehouse or moved there from somewhere else, but he's certainly not fond of being cooped up in Hanson's car, even if he does have the backseat all to himself. Nope, the barking and whining is definitely making it hard to hear and certainly isn't helping put Kitsune's mind at rest.

"As far as I can tell, he's physically fine," I repeat into my cell.

"He sounds so upset though," Kitsune replies, their voice barely audible over the noise.

I sigh. "Okay, look, I'll give you more detail about what's been happening when I get there, but he's going to be shaken for a while. For what it's worth, your name calmed him down a bit. If that's any indication, he'll be a lot better when we get there."

"Do you mean my real name?"

"Yeah, sorry. I kept my voice down, so I don't think anyone heard it." I turn to Hanson, who's keeping a remarkably good sense of humour about Fish's outbursts, and ask, "Did *you* hear what I said to Fish?"

"Nope," she replies, cheerily.

"No, no," Kitsune cuts in. "There's no issue, I was just thinking that it made sense. My real name gets used more around him when we're relaxing. I think he sort of understands the difference between a public and private face. Can you put me on speaker? I might be able to calm him down a little."

"Sure," I say, and tap the speaker button. "You're up."

"Hey, Fish," Kitsune says, using the sort of cheery tone I've heard parents use to distract young children. "Are you coming home now?"

Fish immediately stops barking and sits bolt upright, his ears pricking up.

"Are you being a good boy?"

Now fully recognising Kitsune's voice, Fish starts yipping in response. It's a happier sound than he's been making, but it still has an edge of panic to it.

"I know, I know," Kitsune soothes, choking up a little. "It's okay. You're coming home now."

I hear a quiet *pitter-pattering* behind Fish's response and tilt my head around him. "Ah, shit."

"What's happened?" Kitsune asks.

"Fish just pissed in the car," Hanson replies, checking the rearview mirror and screwing her face up at the sight of the expanding puddle.

"Oh, God, I'm so sorry! You make sure you let me know what it costs to clean, and I'll foot the bill."

"Much appreciated," Hanson replies, and I switch the phone back to normal.

"We're almost with you now. As you can hear, Lieutenant Hanson is with us, so you may want to get your show face on if you haven't already. Oh, and I'd recommend getting as many familiar things ready as you can too. Give Fish something nice to come home to."

"Of course. And thank you, Cassie. Truly."

I smile. "Don't worry about it. We'll be with you in five minutes." I hang up the phone and turn to Hanson, my nose finally catching the smell. "Sorry."

WHEN WE ARRIVE at the theatre, Kevin Smitt is waiting outside the tour bus, his face full of concern. That's a new look for him. I open the door and get out, thankful for the clean air, and open the door to the back-passenger side. Fish jumps out of the car with a bark and tears over to Kevin. He jumps up and starts to shower him with doggy kisses, and Kevin gives him a little fuss before pointing him in through the open tour bus door. Tail wagging like crazy, Fish runs straight in to search for Kitsune.

"Sorry," Kevin says, looking up as I walk over. "We thought it may be better if Fish came home while Kitsune was in *private* mode rather than show mode."

"Makes sense," I say. "Did you want me to come back later to talk through what happened?"

"That would probably be for the best. Look, I caught something on one of the news sites. Apparently, there was a dogfight going on in an old warehouse. Was that where you found him?"

"I can't believe the press are there already." I groan. "But yeah, it was."

"Okay. In that case, it's definitely a good idea to come back later. Kitsune's fragile right now, and that piece of information may be a bit of a shock. I'll make sure the news reports remain off until you get the chance to come back. I'd imagine you have a lot of paperwork to complete at your end anyway. Did I hear that Fish messed in the car too?" I nod, and Kevin waves over to Hanson, who's been examining her backseat since we arrived. "Sorry about that. To reiterate what Kitsune said, we'll pay for the cleaning cost."

Hanson waves gratefully and nods back to the car, signalling that I need to come over. "I'll call later," I tell Kevin and make my way back. "The press is there already," I say when I reach Hanson.

"So I'm told. That's not Kitsune, is it?"

"No, that's Kevin Smitt, Kitsune's manager. The fox is in the bus, but without their mask, so they can't come near the public. Ironclad contracts, right?"

"Fair enough. Did you need to stick it out here, or do you fancy giving me a hand?"

"Smitt's sent me away until later anyway, so sure. I should warn you, though, I don't have a clue how to clean car seats."

Hanson smiles and rolls her eyes. "Nah, we've got people for that. I just had a call from the station saying that, given the suspect's escape from the scene, we need to go fishing for him. We're pretty close to his apartment anyway, so I said I'd go check it out. It shouldn't be a problem, but you know what they say in the ads; you never know what you'll find in New Hopeland. Backup wouldn't be a bad idea, just in case, right?"

"Whaddya reckon?" I ask, glancing up to Bert, who is perched quite comfortably on the roof of the car. "You up for one more?"

Bert gives a *caw* of consent and I smile at Hanson.

CASTLEFORD LIVES IN a mid-price second-floor studio apartment a few blocks from North Main Street that appears to be run by a small team of in-house dogsbodies and handymen. If he's been working for *a lot* of people like Charlie said, then he's either not getting paid the standard Underground rates or he's decided to live comfortably but save his money. Either way, the staff has no issue with confirming that there are windows into the room on the East wall of the building and seem to have no problem with the idea of me sending Bert scurrying up the outer brickwork. With Bert heading upwards to glare menacingly through the thin glass just in case Castleford is already there, the caretaker escorts us up the stairs and tries less than subtly to prise the main purpose of our visit out of Lieutenant Hanson. Hanson is about as receptive to his digging as vampires are to sunlight. On the positive side, he still opens the door for us, even without our telling him what he wanted. Saves me having to add another notch to my doors-kicked-in-post.

Seeing that he's beginning to get under Hanson's skin with his constant jumping between questions and tales of how he should be paid half the staff's wages, I dismiss Mr. Fixes-Everything-In-This-Place with a nod towards Bert at the window and a, "We'll take it from here."

"Well now," Hanson says, tossing me a pair of standard issue rubber gloves. "Looks like someone's been a bit careless, doesn't it?"

She's right. The room is tidy, almost abnormally so. The bedroom area features an immaculately made bed and two cheap clothing units that are essentially thin metal frames hidden inside coloured plastic covers. The kitchen has everything in its place, and a glance into the only separate room, the bathroom, shows a similar degree of crazy cleanliness. The living room features a single couch in front of a large television, with only a coffee table to bridge the gap between them. And therein is the one bit of apparent carelessness: a hybrid laptop tablet with the screen darkened but the standby light flashing, sitting next to a small wad of papers.

"It's very...obvious, isn't it?" I ask.

"Yeah. Which begs the question, is it intentional or was he just in a rush?"

"My guess? Everything on there directly incriminates Allen Fuerza."

Hanson sits down on the couch, picks up the top sheet of paper, and smiles. She waves it towards me and says, "Score one for Cassie. Message print, instructing Castleford to move ahead with *the event*."

"But we know that's not true."

"No, in fairness, what we know is that Fuerza *says* it's not true. He could be covering his tracks, or he could be trying to set Castleford up for some reason. That he won't come in to talk to us himself doesn't help dispel the idea."

I sit down next to Hanson and start reading through the sheet of paper myself, adding, "I said I got the impression he wouldn't come in to talk it through himself, not that he definitely wouldn't. If the stuff here puts him in the picture, I don't see that he would have much choice."

"True enough," Hanson replies, and she reaches out to power up the tablet. The screen flashes into life, not password protected, and opens up straight onto a file containing what appears to be directions. "Probably for the Gloves," Hanson mumbles.

I shake my head and sigh. "I heard Castleford gets pretty busy. There's no way he'd get that much work if he's this lax with security."

"Busy or not, most accountants do a better job of keeping their shit safe than this." She flicks the screen back into standby and folds it down over the keyboard. "I figured it would be pretty unlikely he'd turn up unless he was a complete idiot. *This* is too stupid to be as straightforward as it's obviously meant to look, which means that he at least *thinks* he's being clever. Either that or I'm completely misjudging this. I say we gather what we can and get it back to the station. If it's real, we'll go after Fuerza. If it's not, we'll get our evidence and ramp it up on Castleford."

"Sounds good to me. You guys gonna need some help with it all?"

Hanson shrugs. "Couldn't tell ya. Dev'll probably say yes with the dog papers, but how much we can keep you in the loop with the deep stuff is up in the air. As far as the higher-ups are gonna be concerned, bar the statements we'll need about what happened before we got there, your official involvement ended the moment you got the dog back to its owner. I only suggested you coming along on this because I figured you'd want to. Well, that and because I could. There's a big difference between assisting with a retrieval and actually digging through the stuff. Unless you have a direct involvement with things going forward for reasons beyond our control, of course, like with the Redwood case. Either way, the first thing we need to do is dump the idiot's tablet with the tech guys so they can work their magic and get us some stuff to actually work with."

I nod because I expected that. I'm still certain that Castleford *is* the one behind it, mostly because both Fuerza and Sunglasses didn't set off enough of a warning signal for me to not believe them. Still, I'll take what I can get. "Dev, huh? You mean Corporal Devereaux, right?"

"Yup."

"Since when did you start calling him Dev?"

"Since I found out it pisses him off."

IT'S NEARING MIDNIGHT by the time I get home, and I can't say it's been a fun evening.

Déjà vu is defined as the feeling of already having experienced the present situation. For some, it forms part of the argument that precognition and psychic abilities exist. For others, it's a simple phenomenon that can be explained away as a brain glitch whereby our internal storage system stutters and accidentally files the recognition of the event happening in front of you in the little drawer marked as *past events*. For me, déjà vu is part of living in New Hopeland.

If you stay here long enough, you start to see swathes of similar people doing similar things. When you're in my line of work, that means common case types are usually accompanied by the feeling that I can accurately predict things like motives and behavioural patterns. In a way, it stops being déjà vu and becomes PI's intuition. It's also pretty dangerous because, while many criminals *do* follow the same well-worn paths with far less variance than they *think* they're applying, there will always be someone who'll surprise you. Get yourself into too much of a comfortable pattern and you'll either miss something important or fall into some sort of stupid trap. I learned that from my Dad, way back when I was starting out back in Vancouver. He was worried I was treading the same ground too much and that I'd build up habits I wouldn't be able to shake. Given that he was responsible for passing most of my early cases to me, it was kinda his fault, at least in part. But hey, my Dad was a good man and a good cop, so I was happy for the advice.

Tonight, I'm bored with déjà vu. Step one, interrupting the actual dogfight. After that came repeating the event in detail to a PD interviewer with a video camera that was so new and fancy he forgot to introduce himself and settled straight into fawning all over the little box of plastic and video memories. Next, I made my way back to Kitsune to go through things all over again, albeit in less detail. They were actually closer to home for me and *should* have been my last stop, but I could feel myself getting tetchy already and I didn't want to let that loose on an innocent client. So, Charlie got the brunt of my mood instead. It wasn't really fair on her, but it's not like she wasn't in a foul mood either. By the time I left, two things had smoothed it all over. From Charlie, her normal mug of perfectly made coffee was enough to calm me. At my end, I made a promise to make sure that Castleford was dealt with.

Déjà vu, eh? After living through the whole mess four times, déjà vu can kiss my ass.

Bert seems happy to be home too. He came with me to the station so that I could transfer what little recording he'd done to their databases. He seemed okay with the first few people who came to see him, but the longer we stayed, the more attention he was getting, and in the end, I think the constant prodding got to him. Usually, I can classify most of his synthesised cries of *caw* as serious, cheeky, bored or protective. Today was the first time I've heard one that sounded exasperated. In the end, I let him come into the interview room to perch on my shoulder. He stayed outside on top of the tour bus back at the theatre but came in to pace the hallway at Charlie's.

I pat his head and say, "The life of a celebrity, eh?"

"Caw."

I consider sending a quick message to Lori to let her know that Fish and Kitsune have been reunited, but quickly decide against it. It's far too late now, and I don't want to risk waking her up. Plus, I deserve a break before I talk through it all again. With nothing else to do, I brush my teeth and get ready for bed, letting the home system know that I don't want my alarm hitting before nine tomorrow. Or today now. I collapse onto the bed and spread myself out over the top of the covers. It's a hot night, and the last thing I want is to be stuck with such an uncomfortable temperature that I can't sleep. Just as that thought hits me, my eyes drift shut. I sigh and let the darkness swallow the gentle *clack-clack* of a gargoyle on patrol.

MORE OFTEN THAN not, I'm aware when I'm dreaming. It's the logical part of my brain that does it. *There are no monsters other than those you share the city with.* That's the most common thing it whispers in my ear during dream time. *These are memories* is another. Tonight, it's saying three words: *Isn't it obvious?*

Turning on the spot, I can see that I'm in an old-style newspaper printing office. And by old style, I mean really old style. There's even a small selection of movable type presses. These things are the original Gutenbergs, where staff had to manually use the press rather than rely on steam engines like the later models. I also notice I'm not only wearing the same clothes I've spent the entirety of my less-than-excellent adventure in dogfighting in, but I also appear to be sporting the black and white shading of 1940s cinema.

"You can tell when you've spent too long without a break when your brain decides to go film noir on you," I grumble to myself. It does at least mean that my brain is right, though.

Yes, it's obvious that I'm dreaming. The last thing I remember is lying in bed in an old T-shirt and a loose pair of jogging bottoms while Bert sang his claw-on-wood lullaby. While New Hopeland is home to some very strange individuals, I don't think I've ever met one who would sneak into my office, evade Bert, dress me in my work clothes, and then take me to a place that doesn't exist. Newspaper offices in New Hopeland are all small single floors in multi-business buildings and feature nothing but the newest affordable tech. Plus, you'd be hard-pressed to find a Gutenberg anywhere in Utah these days, with even the museums favouring full immersion prehistoric simulations to old lumps of wood and metal. *Full marks to you on the smell, though, Miss Brain. It stinks worse than the time Terry Crawford sprayed ink up my nose in tenth-grade Biology.*

I smile at the memory of trying to jam his leaky fountain pen up his nose in retaliation. Was it worth the detention? Yes, it was.

I walk up to the nearest press and try to read the prearranged letter blocks, but they're all blank. Must be a slow news night.

Thud.

I turn to the third of the printing presses just in time to see the large wooden board at the back slide noisily under the press block. The crank at the top creaks around, pushing the weighted section down, then clatters back again and the board slides back out. The board on the press next to me snaps shut on a sheet of paper I'm sure wasn't there a second ago and slams down onto the printing block, then starts to slide under the press. I take a step back and notice that not only has the other press started the same sequence, but the third press is now repeating the same movements at an unnatural speed, spreading printed paper into the air with each cycle.

I back myself up against the door to the room and give the knob a quick jiggle. Not unexpectedly, it's locked. "Night of the Haunted Printing Press." I groan and step forward into the swirling storm of freshly printed paper. I snatch a couple of pieces out of the air and skim through the matching headlines and articles. The stories all come with two identical and poorly rendered photographs interspersed with the text, which seems ridiculous because I'm pretty sure that the early Gutenbergs were used for text only. Nothing like your brain taking artistic licence to make a point, eh?

The article in question is something that I have a vague recollection of. The PD got a call from someone whose name I can't remember stating that they'd found a body in the middle of the street. Investigations showed that the CCTV for the area had mysteriously shut down for half an hour, and when they returned, the body was suddenly present. The dead man was Johnny something. I know that because the word Johnny is clear on the paper, but the surname is, much like the mystery caller's name, smeared and smudged out. *It's nice to know my memory is as infallible as ever.*

The first photo shows a small number of nameless cops working at the scene, but that's clearly not what my brain is trying to get me to realise. The second photo is the important one because, while a little blurred, it clearly shows that the caller was a younger Sunglasses Paloma. I scratch my head and try to remember the case. It was before I moved here, I think, but not so long before that, it wasn't still buzzing around the sites on a regular basis. That's right... Johnny was supposed to have done something to upset the Kings. I remember because that was the first time I'd heard about them.

The mystery caller disappeared shortly after the case was closed as some sort of accidental death, and the conspiracy nuts all decided he must have been one the King's hitmen or something like that, and he'd just gotten careless and been taken care of. If he fell out with the Kings but didn't find himself six feet under, he must have built up a lot of goodwill with them. Which means a lot of *good* work. Yeah, I was right to be wary around him.

The printing presses stop abruptly, and for a moment the only sound is the gentle rustle of the last few identical sheets fluttering down to the ground. Once they've all fallen, I hear a loud *click* behind me and turn to see the door behind me open into darkness. I shrug, chuck the papers in my hand onto the pile that's amassed in front of me, and walk through the door.

I DON'T KNOW if it was instantaneous, or if I just didn't have any more dreams, but the next thing I remember is the gentle sound of my alarm bleeping unobtrusively through the room speakers. "Alarm off," I grumble, and stretch my arms behind my head, soaking up the comfortable feel of my tense muscles relaxing.

I raise one hand to my face and rub the sleep out of eyes. "Sunglasses worked for the Kings, eh? That's a big fall. Maybe he's planning to use Fuerza to instigate some sort of revenge plot? Either that or his death was a ruse and the Kings want something out of Fuerza. Ugh. Conspiracy Tam at your service. Stupid brain."

A yawn signals the start of my normal routine, but I only get as far as beginning the dressing step before my phone rings. Since meeting Lori, or to be more accurate, since Lori decided that my embarrassment at how I was dressed when I first met her was a good source of fun, I've become a little more careful about making sure I get dressed. It's not that I don't still feel calling at a ridiculous time is justification for having to deal with me as you find me, it's more that I kind of feel like I *should* be saving my natural-if-slightly-slovenly form for Lori. Well, barring accidents anyway. I can't guarantee I'm going to be getting any morning visitors today, but with the number of threads left hanging from the Castleford mess, I can't entirely rule it out. If I thought it was more likely than not that I'd have a company-free morning, then I'd sit down on the bed and answer the phone in my underwear, safe in the knowledge that it's not my fault if someone decides to come knocking entirely unexpected. As it is, there's too great a possibility of unannounced visitors, so I say out loud, "Synch room speakers with telecommunication device one, and begin call transmission. Integrate room tracking, target, Cassandra Tam."

"Synch complete," the system replies. "Transferring call."

After a moment, the ringing cuts off and a short *beep* plays through the room speakers, letting me know I can start chatting. "Cassie Tam," I say, and start to work on untangling the legs on the pair of trousers that I carefully screwed up into a ball and chucked into my closet after the last laundry run.

"Miss Tam," a familiar voice replies. "I trust you are well?"

Dream of the Devil. "Well enough."

"We understand there were some complications with Mr. Castleford's arrest," Sunglasses Paloma replies. His voice is eerily calm, making what he's said a simple statement of fact rather than an attempt at confirmation.

"You *could* say that. You know I can't tell you too much, though, eh?"

"Of course. If we understand the situation on a base level, however, we may be able to offer some assistance."

I sigh and slip my legs into the trousers. "The dogfight was just starting when I got there. I made sure it didn't go ahead, but Castleford got away before the cops arrived. Is Fuerza there with you?"

"I am afraid not."

"Okay, well, would he be willing to speak to the police about what's been happening?"

"We would rather avoid that, unless absolutely necessary, Miss Tam. Mr. Fuerza and the New Hopeland Law Enforcement Agencies do not see eye to eye."

"Don't see eye to eye? That's an understatement. Look, I went to Castleford's apartment with one of the officers that was part of the raid. He wasn't there, but his laptop was."

"I see. And would I be correct in assuming that he had set this up in order to place the blame for the dogfight on Mr. Fuerza?"

There's no point in showing your cards just yet, Cassie. Especially when you're not far from an empty hand here. "I couldn't tell you. But until the PD tech guys get through with it, I doubt they'll make a move on Castleford. Should I expect them to find anything implicating your boss?"

"I suspect you already know the answer to this, Miss Tam. However, in the spirit of playing along, neither you nor the police will find anything legitimate. Whether that fact can be proven will be key to the smooth conclusion of this debacle."

"I don't like the way you said smooth."

"And we do not like the possibility that there will be any other form of conclusion. Needless to say, we are prepared for any eventuality."

I finish buttoning my shirt but put off rummaging for a tie. "What happens if the PD find out something about this secret of Fuerza's? It sounds like you're preparing for war here."

"It is not our belief that they will. The nature of the information Mr. Castleford obtained is such that revealing it in this way would do nothing to further his probable goal. In that respect, we expect him not to have stored anything on the systems at his known residential locations. It is more likely that he has a further storage point, but we cannot be certain of this. Regardless, the publication of the aforementioned information would be nothing more than a desperation move on his part."

"You're not going to tell me what he found either, are you?"

"No. Even if I thought it was going to be useful to you, you would be better off not knowing. Frankly, everyone would."

"*Diu.* If you're not going to tell me anything, then why bother...? Wait. You're worried that he *is* desperate, aren't you? Or that he will be soon."

"Children sometimes argue over the perceived ownership of toys. In some cases, when asked to share, a greedy child will break the toy rather than have to give up part of their time with it."

"If I can't have it, you can't have it either."

"Precisely. Mr. Castleford is ambitious, and his desires match this trait. If desperate enough, we cannot rule out that this will become his mentality."

"You don't strike me as the sort who would avoid killing. I hate to say it, but why not just take him down? That's the way this place normally works."

"I do not kill indiscriminately, Miss Tam. In addition, ambition is a useful trait for employees to have. If you are already at the top of an organisation, you seek to find the best ways to motivate your staff. Ambition is something that is easily manipulated. Despite this slip-up on Mr. Castleford's part, his overriding desires combined with his skills mean that he remains useful to Mr. Fuerza. Providing he can be reined in, of course. His legal capture may serve to remind him of his place."

"And if it doesn't?" Sunglasses remains silent, giving me the answer I expected. Execution isn't uncommon in the New Hopeland Underground. "You said you may be able to be of assistance. How?"

"There are those among his list of victims who wish to make amends for their actions. Then, there are others who find his actions deplorable. While I am confident that any searches of Mr. Castleford's personal possessions will reveal nothing more than easily debunked evidence implicating Mr. Fuerza, it is imperative that his arrest occurs before he can reach a point where he reverts to childlike actions. We are offering to assist in locating Mr. Castleford and herding him to you."

I narrow my eyes and ask, "Why me? If you believe his evidence can be so readily debunked, then why not send him to the police?"

"As I said, Miss Tam, Mr. Fuerza and New Hopeland's finest do not see eye to eye. Given the opportunity, they may simply wish to use insubstantial evidence as a means to capture Mr. Fuerza rather than the actual culprit. You, on the other hand, understand how this works. The police, in particular, must be seen to be standing in the light, even if they are in truth as veiled in shadows as the rest of us. You are in the unique position whereby you stand equally in both light and dark and do not attempt to hide this. You may not know what the big picture is in this case, Miss Tam, but you know there is one."

Ouch. Well, that kinda hurts. I'm no angel, but I'm not half demon either. Fine, let's fire back but keep things moving anyway. "I don't know. No offence, but Fuerza isn't exactly the biggest fish in the pond."

"No, but he is a bigger fish than Mr. Castleford." He pauses for a moment, then asks, "Were you able to retrieve your client's dog unharmed?"

"Yeah. Yeah, I was."

"I see. In that case, your involvement with Mr. Castleford is technically at an end. Perhaps then, a different tack is required. If you are willing to ensure that Mr. Castleford is brought to justice, then I can personally guarantee three things. One, you will be allowed to proceed with the case as you see fit. Two, you will have our resources at your disposal as already detailed. And three, providing you do not intentionally falter in the overall goal, Mr. Fuerza will match your previous client's fee or provide a higher figure if more suitable, irrespective of whether we end up having to take more drastic actions."

If I'm being honest, I would have gone ahead with hunting down Castleford anyway. I won't tolerate cruelty to animals. As much as I hate to admit it, the extra money would be good too, even if it means officially throwing in with Fuerza for a while. "Fine." I groan. "Give me some time to find out what the police are up to, and I'll call you back when I know what I need. The number you're calling from isn't withheld, is it?"

"It is; however, I can message you the details. The phone is a burner and will be out of commission at the conclusion of your employment."

"True. In the meantime, keep an eye out for Castleford, but don't act until I'm ready to do something about it."

"Very well, Miss Tam. We will be in touch."

Sunglasses hangs up and within seconds I receive a message confirming the number for the cell he's using. I don't have a clue what could be so important that Allen Fuerza of all people would want me on board for this. All I know for sure is that *he* is an idiot, and Castleford is an unknown quantity. "Better the Devil you know." I sigh and start hunting for a tie.

In the end, I decide on one of my older ones. Much like most of my collection, it's a shiny black with a solid black design embossed on it, barely visible unless you get up close. This one has two bats crossing in the air. It's an odd-looking design, but there's a reason for picking it. The Chinese word for bat is pronounced the same as the word for good fortune. In folklore, one bat means good luck, and two means doubly good luck. I'm not as superstitious as some of my family, but I get the feeling I'm gonna need a lot of luck to pull this off. Especially as I'm about to test the big fish, bigger fish theory.

I hit the speed dial for the station and the phone rings twice before someone answers, "New Hopeland PD."

"Hey. Can I speak to Lieutenant Hanson?"

"Uh...she's just heading towards the door. Who's calling?"

"Cassie Tam. It's about the dogfight."

"Ah, the raid yesterday. Hold on."

I hear the familiar scrape of a hand covering the receiver, and the nameless desk jockey starts shouting something in the background. It's muffled, but I can just about make out my name being yelled twice. Eventually, Hanson comes on the line and asks, "Cassie? Is this important? I'm just about to head out on...something."

"Fuerza just hired me to make sure Castleford is arrested."

"Shit." Hanson sighs. "Hang on."

Hanson says something to the first guy and, after a moment, the phone beeps and Hanson comes back on. "Okay, I'm at my desk. What's going on?"

"Fair trade. I'll tell you the latest, then I need to know why you're heading to Fuerza's."

"That obvious, huh? Fine, fine. What've you got?"

"Fuerza's certain that whatever you find on Castleford's gear will be easily disproven. He's worried that, once that comes to light, Castleford is going to get desperate and spill the reason he's trying to frame him. No, before you ask, I still don't know what it is Castleford dug up, but Fuerza clearly doesn't want it getting out. The guy I've been speaking to thinks it would be better for *everyone* if they didn't know."

"Which makes it clear that Fuerza's hiding something."

"And so is every other crook in the city. Fuerza *is* running scared, though. He doesn't want Castleford to have the chance to spread whatever he has to the rest of the Underground, and he doesn't want the PD to decide *he's* worth more behind bars than the accountant and just act on Castleford's files without acknowledging that they can be disproven."

"He is, Cassie."

"I'm sorry?"

"Fuerza. He *is* worth more behind bars than Castleford. When did you last hear of Fuerza doing time?"

I think about that for a moment and say, "I don't know. Why?"

"Because he hasn't *ever* been convicted. He's on the lowest rung of the criminal food chain, yet he's never been sent down. Usually, you have to be a lot better connected to manage that, but he seems to have gotten by simply by not getting caught in anything big enough to warrant us swarming him. Even his hitmen-for-hire racket is such a joke that no one's gonna take it seriously. That's the problem. What you've just said makes it sound like we might finally be able to dig something up to justify getting him off the streets."

"But that wasn't why you were going there, was it? What did you turn up on Castleford's files?"

Hanson laughs and says, "A deal's a deal. Do you know what onion routing is?"

"Yeah, we covered it at the academy. One message gets sent, and each time it reaches its destination, a layer is stripped away, leaving the instructions as to where to send it next. It was an old system designed to mask recipients, but it's not untraceable."

"Right. Don't knock it being an old system, though, it's still widely used. Anyway, the messages Castleford received were put through the onion routing system, and traffic reports point to them originating from a computer in Fuerza's building. But like you said yourself, having the message printed out and waiting for us was too tidy. We had one of the Monitoring Office guys take a look at the message."

"The GMO, huh? And what did they say?"

"There are indicators that the message was auto-generated. To prove it, we need access to the machine that sent the message. To be honest with you, Cassie, the plan was to grab what we need and go hunting for Castleford. While I'd love to have an excuse to take Fuerza in, if for no other reason than that his turn is long overdue, the GMO involvement means that we can't just ignore the evidence."

"If you're that set on Fuerza, you could have just accepted the print out as a slip-up."

"Nah, you know me. I get the idea of the *right* result not always being the *accurate* one, but unless it's something major, I'll stick with the truth. The thing is, from what you've said, there's a lot more going here. But I doubt we'll dig *that* up on his systems. The problem now is how we approach it going forward. If this really is as big as Fuerza's making out, at least for *him*, Castleford going public could cause some major chaos. I doubt anyone would care about our favourite wannabe crime lord getting shut down, but..." She sighs. "We did some digging and you were right about him being busy. If he sells out Fuerza, there are a lot of people in a lot of different places who are going to start panicking that he's gonna do the same to them."

Time to take the lead, Cassie. "Is there any way you could check the auto-generated thing without physically taking Fuerza's computer away?"

Hanson clicks her tongue. "Well, we know what we're looking for now. I guess I could bring a tech guy with me, but that wouldn't be the normal procedure. Why?"

"Think of it as a gesture of goodwill. I can get Fuerza to let you take a look at his stuff willingly, which will save you a lot of time and effort, but I doubt he'll want it all taken away somewhere it can be tampered with. Letting him have someone present to make sure you're only looking at what you need to will make him more likely to cooperate. Then, when you have your proof that Castleford set it all up..."

"I put an APB out on him," Hanson cuts in.

"Not immediately."

"No? Why not?"

"Fuerza thinks he'll panic, remember? Look, Fuerza's already got some guys looking for Castleford for me. I'll get Castleford to the station, I promise, but if he hears that every cop in the state is after him, it increases the chances that he'll either go public or disappear entirely."

"Cassie, if we get the evidence, then I can't avoid putting the APB out unless we already have him in custody."

"Then don't avoid it, delay it. Give me some time."

"Hold on," Hanson replies, and her voice goes quiet as she speaks to someone else in the station. I barely make out something about how long the scans will take but can't quite hear the response. Then, she brings the phone back to her mouth. "The techs say that, depending on how straightforward Fuerza's systems are, it'll take between one and three hours to get what we need. Speak to Fuerza, make sure he cooperates, and I'll delay putting the APB out until I get back here. With travel and rearranging the team going with me, that gives you six hours, max. After that, we'll be hitting every address you gave us."

"Deal. Thanks, Hanson."

"Don't mention it. Just don't be slow," she says and hangs up.

Chapter Eight

"FINE," FUERZA GRUNTS, his voice distorting slightly on the phone line. "I wouldn't have had a problem with the police taking the machine, though. What would be the point? Or do you think I'd be stupid enough to leave important files on something so easy to access?"

Read important as confirmation of illegal activity. "Yes," I reply. "Yes, I do think you'd be that stupid."

I hear a sharp intake of breath over the receiver and smile. What can I say? Right now, Fuerza is using me as a gofer. Not only that, but my earlier conversation with Sunglasses made it quite clear that he likes to manipulate situations more than I gave him credit for. I reserve my right to torment anyone who thinks they can use me, even if they *are* paying me for the privilege. Time is ticking, though, so I continue, "That's not why I told them you'd want the testing done on site. I've worked with Lieutenant Hanson before, and there was no way she was going to just give me free rein on this. Buying time was always going to be the best I could do and having her staying at the opposite end of the city from the station was the easiest way to maximise that."

Fuerza growls in frustration. "I don't care what your reasons were, it's going to be a pain in the ass having the cops crawling around here. If you weren't the best option we had to avoid any other potential betrayals without bloodshed, then I'd..."

"You'd what, Mr. Fuerza?" I cut in, putting a small snap in my voice.

Fuerza takes a deep breath in and exhales slowly. The phone rattles and the next voice I hear belongs to Sunglasses. "Mr. Fuerza has left to take care of the necessary arrangements for our impending visit from Lieutenant Hanson and her team."

"He doesn't like it when he's not in control, does he?"

"He does not take kindly to direct challenges, perhaps *because* he is aware of his standing in the New Hopeland hierarchy. Tell me, Miss Tam, if you were not aware of who Allen Fuerza is, would you still be so eager to antagonise him?"

I frown. "What the hell kinda question is that?"

"Let us call it a consideration for the future."

You, Sunglasses Paloma, are a strange one. "I guess it depends on what I *did* know. If all I knew was his job description and the hype he gives himself, maybe not. Unless he deserved it. Given that I'm half devil, though, who can tell."

"I see, so that is how you inferred my earlier statement. To clarify, Miss Tam, I am under no illusions as to your nature. You are not one of the Underground, not truly. I simply meant you are in a position that allows you to bridge the gap between both sides of the New Hopeland law system. You are not the only PI in the city, nor are you the only person positioned ethically on the side of the justice system who has worked alongside those who oppose it in some way. It is your standing, your accumulated results, and your rigid stance on your own moral beliefs that allows you to straddle both sides of the divide."

"Except I don't recall working for any criminals before today."

"Trust me, Miss Tam. You have resolved cases for many that are under Fuerza's control, though they themselves would never say so."

Well, that's *good to know. Maybe I should start background checking more of my clients. Let's just try to get this over with.* "We're wasting time here. Have your guys had any luck in locating Castleford?"

"Not as yet, though we haven't checked the full list of potential hideouts yet."

"Are there any near me? I'm at my office right now."

He thinks for a moment then confirms, "Block thirteen, Faraday Mall is near to you, I believe. He often stops at the patisserie in that section of the complex. We have not sent anyone to look as yet, as he will be aware he is currently under suspicion. Unless he is given indication that he is no longer in such a predicament, we do not believe him likely to be relaxing with a cake at this time."

"Seems reasonable. The way he acted during the raid makes me think he knew it would happen, though. He's arrogant enough to think his plan is foolproof. If I'm right about the raid, he might be banking on your thinking exactly that and be trying to hide in plain sight. Sitting around isn't my style, so as you haven't got anyone else there already, I'll go check it out. If nothing else, it'll give you another place to tick off the list."

"Very well. Will you require transportation? I understand you do not yourself drive."

"Nah, I'll walk it. If I need to get anywhere further away, then I'll see what I can arrange. From what you said, I'm as much an enemy as I am an ally to you guys, so I'd rather not risk finding out what you'd do if everything goes to Hell before I can catch Castleford."

"Paranoia," Sunglasses says, labelling my habit with more admiration than I expected. "It's more useful than those with simpler lives understand."

"Let me know if you find anything," I say, avoiding getting into an unnecessary conversation. "If I need somewhere else to visit, I'll call you."

I hang up and head back to my *working clutter* drawer. After a bit of rummaging, I pull out the photo of Castleford that Sunglasses supplied yesterday and glance over at the handgun resting next to the files. After his refusal to back down from the dog yesterday, I'm reluctant to take Bert into a large group of people. I understand why he acted the way he did, but insubordination at the wrong time won't bode well for anyone. Besides, even on the off chance I *do* find Castleford, I should just be dealing with him this time. If things look like they're gonna get out of hand, I have an emergency summoning command on my phone anyway.

I check the gun is loaded, grab two spare cartridges, and head back into the living room area of the apartment. Gun laws are such that you see a lot of people carrying them these days, but it's policed well enough that we rarely have any trouble. The general rules of thumb are that criminal record equals no gun licence and those carrying keep them holstered and covered but in clear sight. I start strapping my holster to my belt and turn to my shiny little friend. "Hey, Bert. I'm gonna head to the mall. I need you to stay here for this one. D'ya think you can manage to not wreck the place while I'm out?"

"Caw. Caw."

I roll my eyes and pat his shiny head. "That's what I thought. If I run into trouble, I'll call you in."

"Caw."

I nod and walk out of the office, locking the door behind me. If I call him, Bert'll exit through the window. The only reason I've left all of them shut right now is I don't want to risk him continuing his disobedience and following me. If I can put yesterday down to a single behavioural blip or a necessary overriding effect in his programming, that's fine. Too many issues in a short space of time would mean another trip to the factory, though, and I'd rather not have to consider having his personality reset. He's a cheeky, destructive little ball of spite at times, but I wouldn't have him any other way.

MOST PLACES I'VE visited have dedicated shopping streets that serve as haunts for the fashionable elite. They're filled with overpriced representations of whatever we are, as a species, told we should like for the next five minutes. Malls, as a rule, tend to get the occasional outlet store for a big name brand but otherwise fill the clothing areas with a focus on the affordable. It's different here, though. Maybe it's the shiny exterior or the ever-changing digital advertising boards, but when New Hopeland's Faraday Mall was built, the high-end retailers flocked like the magpies of European superstition, all eager to steal their little bit of sparkly store space. The result of that is that shoppers with more money in loose change than I have in my bank prowl the mall like foxes, as they try to decide which bird to throw themselves at.

My grandfather once told me that magpies are good luck, so as much as the far-too-rich snobbery of the shoppers is making me wish I was in the founding era of the city when 90 percent of it was industrial, I'm keeping my hopes up. If Malcolm Castleford's delusions of grandeur are enough to make him want to hang out with the upper classes of the city, then he may well be hiding out among the masses. So, I pull out the photo and show it to a woman who, from her expression, wasn't aware that something as low class as physical paper still existed. "Excuse me, Madame, but I was wondering if you may have seen this man at all? His name is Malcolm Castleford and his presence is required at the police station."

"I see. And *you* work for the police, do you?" she replies, her voice dripping with disgust.

"*With* them," I clarify. "I'm a Private Investigator. Have you..."

She cuts me off with a snort and says, "A Private Investigator? So, someone who simply wasn't good enough to become a proper policewoman, then. Well, that doesn't surprise me at all. If you were any good at your job, you'd already know that someone like me wouldn't be seen in public with some *criminal.*"

"Is that so?" I smile sweetly. "I notice you've decided he *must* be a criminal, though, which completely disregards the possibility he could be a witness to a crime who's just too scared to come forward willingly. But then, maybe you've got a good eye for criminals. You did say you wouldn't be seen in *public* with one, but there are plenty of non-public places about, eh? Your bedroom, perhaps?"

Was that a little unnecessary? Yes. Was it worth it to see the woman turn so red that I expect smoke to come out of her ears before she storms off? Absolutely. Unfortunately, the next few shoppers I approach are equally as unhelpful. If I had more time, I'd try to get access to the security footage again, but given how big this place is, I'd need a full team to go through it. So, I switch tack and start questioning the floor staff in the men's stores selling similar suits to the one Castleford was wearing when I saw him last. By the time I come out of the fifth store, I'm about ready to give up.

"Excuse me, my dear."

I turn towards the voice and see an elderly lady sitting on a bench in front of the store. With her curled grey hair, slightly over-sized glasses, shoulder shawl, and walking stick, she's about as close to the typical granny as you can get. She smiles at me and pats the spot next to her. *Well, it's not like I couldn't do with a quick break.*

I sit down and return the smile, and the woman says, "You know, when you reach my age, you really need a hobby, or the days just start to run into each other. Me, I quite enjoy people watching. This place is always full of so many people that it's a virtual paradise for it. Well now, I've been people watching today, and do you know what I've seen? I've seen you running up and down showing passersby a photograph and asking if they've seen someone."

"Good hearing," I comment.

"Of course, dear, I'm old, not deaf. Now, let's see. You're Cassie Tam, aren't you?"

I blink and let out a little laugh. "I guess you must have seen one of the news reports."

"Yes, but that wasn't where I recognised you from. We're quite a closed community up on Forster Street, you see, and we've all sort of adopted young Miss Redwood as our token reminder of our youth. Jennifer Albright," she says and offers a hand.

I shake it and smile but, to quote Lori at the start of this whole mess, feel totally spied upon now. "I don't think I've seen you up there before?" I try, a little more nervously than I'd like.

"Oh, you wouldn't, dear. I'm a fair bit subtler than Edna. That's the lady who lives next door to Lori. Ah, but Lori does speak fondly of you. So, as I've been here all day thus far, how about you show me that photograph of yours and I'll see if I can help at all."

"Sure," I reply and pull it back out of my pocket. I pass it over and the old lady nods a few times, humming some old tune to herself.

"Yes. Yes, I know that one. He's not been around today, at least not that I've noticed, but he has a storage locker near my own. Is he in some sort of trouble? He's not what I would call talkative, so I wouldn't really know what to make of him."

"He could be," I reply. "If I don't find him, he could be in even more trouble."

"Hmm. Would it be of use if I were to show you to his locker? I know the code if it's needed."

"That might help a lot, actually. But...how do you know his code?"

Jennifer Albright winks and says, "I'm old, dear, not blind."

I laugh and push to my feet. *Looks like I'm gonna have to be extra careful up on Forster Street from now on.*

THERE ARE SEVERAL sets of storage lockers in the New Hopeland Mall, with multiple sitting on each floor. They can be used for personal storage, or you can set them up as pseudo-PO boxes for deliveries from online companies if you don't want items delivered to your home. The adverts say they're ideal for surprise birthday presents and so on, but the more cynical people of the city say they're even better for receiving and storing items you don't want your partner knowing about.

By the time we reach the lockers at the back of the first floor, I've learned that Mrs. Albright is ninety years old, and lives with her husband Gary, who is five years her junior. He is apparently only absent today because he's off helping to promote a charity boxing event over in Ogden. Oh, and in her own words, Mrs. Albright is well aware of personal boundaries with her spying on people, she just doesn't much care for them.

Anyway, just as she promised, Mrs. Albright taps in a code, confirming it as "A-A-7-9-D-8" as she goes, and Castleford's locker clicks open. The smell that creeps out gets instant recognition from me; the sewers. It's not as strong as when you're actually down there, but it's bad enough. Mrs. Albright seems unfazed. *Maybe her sense of smell is leaving her out of jealousy for her sight and hearing.*

I cover my mouth and nose with one hand and reach into the locker. At first it appears to be empty, but then, right at the back, I find something only a little bigger than my hand. I pull the item out and turn away from the still open locker. It's a small motherboard, loaded with a small processor, a memory card, a wireless network adapter, and a small light display. Both lights on the poorly soldered attachment are lit up red.

"What is it?"

I glance at the inquisitive old lady and reply, "Honestly? I don't have a clue."

"Ah, that's a shame, dear. I'm sorry I can't be more help."

"No, no, you've saved me a lot of time. Thank you."

"Quite all right dear," she says. "Well, I'm going to get back to my people watching. If I happen to see your missing person, I'll be sure to call you on the number on your website."

"Thank you. That'd be appreciated."

"Not at all," Mrs. Albright replies and starts shuffling away, leaving me to stare at the strange electronic device in my hand. The motherboard, processor and memory card mean it's running some sort of system, and the adapter means it's transmitting. From the lights, it obviously has a power source too, though I can't see it. *Maybe it's built into one of the attachments?*

The problem now is what to do with it. I don't want to risk leaving it here, just in case it's important and Castleford comes back and destroys it. At the same time, if he comes back and finds it missing, he may react badly, which is what I'm trying to avoid. Unfortunately, that means I'm going to have to put it back for now and hope my luck holds. As I reach into the locker, the smell hits me again, but it's much weaker this time. I frown. *It's dissipating pretty quickly. Come to think of it, Charlie didn't mention the stink on me when she found me in her basement either. She could be used to it, or maybe it just...*

I push the locker door shut and lean back against it, facing out into the mall. *The locker must be airtight, or someone would have caught the smell escaping before now. Either he had the thing down in the sewers with him, or he got here pretty quickly to check on it after leaving the sewers. That would mean...*

I grab my cell and dial Charlie's number. She answers after four rings. "Caz? Is it important? I'm about to head out to try to sort this Castleford mess."

"Yeah, me too, I think. Don't worry, I'll be quick. Do you know if *all* the supply tunnels open out into the sewers?"

"Most of them do, why?"

"I'm chasing a hunch here," I say, ignoring the question, "but would I be right that you don't get much wireless connectivity down there?"

Charlie sighs and replies, "You do if you're close to a property, but we have systems to monitor hot spots like that. Outside of those areas, it's about as good as it is in the sewers, so weak if at all."

"Okay, last question. Is there a supply tunnel entrance in the New Hopeland Mall?"

"You think he's still down there, don't you?"

"Maybe, but I don't know if he's more likely to be in the tunnels themselves or the sewers."

Charlie goes quiet for a moment then says, "I'll make some calls and get the Sweepers to box him in."

I close my eyes and tap my hand nervously against the lockers. The Sweepers are the hired security for the Dealers. They're efficient enough to be offered other jobs, but the Dealers get priority for their time, even if it means cutting other stuff short. They're also pretty scary, which makes them a risk here. Not to mention that boxing someone in is usually the first step towards putting them in a box. "Thanks, but I don't think the Sweepers are the best way to handle this."

"Why?" Charlie asks slowly.

"Because my new client thinks that if he's cornered, then Castleford's likely to let loose with something that would be bad for everyone. I don't know what Castleford has, but I believe my client on this one."

Charlie sighs. "I don't think you understand what's at stake here, Caz. If he's gone AWOL with the intent of spilling the details of..." She swallows audibly and continues, "I'm pretty clean personally, but there are enough things going on that all of the Dealers would be dragged down if it came down to it."

"And if I told you I think he's only after my client?"

"Who's the client?" When I don't immediately answer, she repeats, sternly, "Who is your client?"

"Allen Fuerza."

"Jesus, Caz! Who the Hell has anything to gain from dicking with Allen Fuerza?"

"I believe him, Charlie."

Charlie groans. "Your instincts are normally good on stuff like this, but you're so, so wrong on this one."

"And what if I'm not?"

"You are."

"But what if I'm not? Then what will you do? Execute someone needlessly?"

Charlie is silent for a moment, then asks, "You're really certain about this, aren't you?"

"Yeah, I am."

"If there's any chance he's going to be publicising something potentially dangerous, then I have to assume the worst and tell the others. I'm sorry, Caz, but there's no way I can avoid that, the risk is too great. This is gonna be a tough hour. For both of us. Just...just don't go looking for a janitor's closet at the back of the surplus stock storeroom at the back of the Mall."

She hangs up before I can thank her, and I start moving, dialling Sunglasses as I go. "Miss Tam?" he answers after a single ring.

"I've screwed up. I'm pretty sure he's either in the sewers or one of the Dealer Supply Tunnels near the Mall, but the Elites are gonna send the Sweepers in. If he's in the right place, he'll still be able to send whatever he wants wherever he wants."

"How long until they reach him?"

"An hour, I think. Maybe a little more. If there's any way you can keep them off my back..."

"That won't be a problem. I'll track your location and ensure that you don't run into any unnecessary obstacles."

"Track my location? How?"

"The message I sent with the number for this phone contained a small file. That installed a tracker on your phone. Don't worry, it will delete itself once this handset is destroyed."

No time to get annoyed about that one, Cassie. Keep moving. "Fine." I grunt and hang up.

THE STOREROOM AT the back of the mall is as large as a small modern warehouse, but the closet Charlie mentioned is easy enough to find. Once I remember the tracks on the bottom of the generator in the sewer entrance, it becomes equally as simple to find the table that operates the door mechanism. I crawl through the small opening and come out into a room even smaller than the janitor's closet. It's well lit and surprisingly clean given that the only thing in the room, a manhole cover, likely leads down into the murky depths.

Moving with urgency, I haul the cover open and drop down onto the ladder below, taking the first the few rungs quickly before stalling to pull the cover back into place. What can I say? My parents always said to leave things the way I found them. That and if he isn't down here and does come this way, I don't want him to realise he's not alone. I hit the bottom of the ladder and give my surroundings a quick glance. The area looks almost identical to the Western sewer tunnels, which means poor, albeit marginally better, lighting, but not too many offshoot paths. I can't get to the other side of the swirling mess of stench and miscellaneous excrement without wading through it and Castleford shouldn't be that desperate yet. Or I hope he's not anyway. That stuff smells worse than the last lot, somehow.

"A Bert, a Bert, my Glock for a Bert," I mutter, passing the third side turning without any way of knowing whether I should check down it or not. He would have been a risk in the Mall, but his tracking skills would have been great down here. "Shame it'd take him too long to get here now."

I keep moving forward and pass another two tunnels, all the while muttering to myself about what I think I'm doing down here. I need to think of something because right now I'd be doing just as well standing still and waiting for him to come to me. If it weren't for the combination of the smell and what I just saw floating by in the *water*, I'd be tempted. With a sigh, I keep moving on until I come to a metal bridge. *Well, that's just great. Now which way do I go?*

Up until now, I was safe in the knowledge that Castleford could only have gone one of two ways, forward or down one of the turnings I skipped. This means that his options are now forward, down a side tunnel, forward on the other side, back on the other side, or down a side tunnel on the other side. If I was right that he came down here at all. "I can't just stand here." I groan and start walking out onto the bridge. "Maybe I've fallen into a TV show and he'll have conveniently dropped something to give me a clue."

Of course, there's nothing on the bridge that can help me. So, I stop and rest on the railings, staring ahead and trying to think. *There's no point in doubling back now, so that leaves going forward. But which side? And do I take any of the tunnels or stick on the main path?*

Up ahead, I can count two tunnels on the right, each illuminated faintly by lighting only a little better than those in the Western sewer tunnels. Still, better at least means I can see them. On the left-hand path, where I've been walking up until now, I count one tunnel that's illuminated. With the way the system is laid out, there should be another tunnel further ahead and in line with the second tunnel on the right, but the lights must be out. I'd say that's weird given the functionality of the other lights, but this is a sewer system, not a five-star hotel. "Whatever." I sigh and start heading back towards the path I was already on. "No lighting is all I've got to go on right now."

I make my way up the walkway until I come to the darkened tunnel and immediately turn down it before I can overthink things and second guess myself. About halfway down, I come to a small generator. There are no tracks under it, so it's not a door mechanism, but there are some extra cables sticking out of the back of it. I take hold of them and follow along in the darkness until they start to reach down to the wall and off down a floor level grate. I squat because screw getting on my hands and knees unless I have to, and peer through the thick metal bars. My view is obscured by something, but there's a dim light at the end of the room and I can hear *something* in the background. A female voice, I think, and one that's sort of familiar. The dark shape ahead of me moves and I realise I'm looking at the silhouette of a pair of shoes.

I smile and stand up. A few more quiet steps ahead, I come to another turning and start making my way up it, keeping my hand on the damp wall for guidance. Partway up the tunnel, I find the entrance to a small room. There are lamps in each corner, providing a little extra illumination to accompany the dim glow of the normal sewer lights. The power cables from each have been daisy-chained around the room towards what looks like a homemade battery pack of some sort. With the haphazard way it's attached to the generator cables, it definitely wouldn't pass a health and safety check. Next to the battery is a faded red armchair pushed up against where the grate should be. The source of the feet silhouette is no longer there, however, because he's stooped over at the other end of the room, giving an old television a series of hard slaps.

The picture stabilises, and the audio comes back. The voice I heard was a news reporter, which is why it sounded familiar. "There," Malcolm Castleford says with a smile. He takes one step backwards, then stops, his smile dropping when he feels the barrel of my Glock pressed against the back of his head.

"Malcolm Castleford," I say, and nudge my gun a little tighter to his head. "Walk slowly forward and place your hands flat against the wall."

Castleford does as he's told and doesn't flinch when I start to frisk him for any weapons. "You don't sound familiar," he says. "Hired from the outside, I assume?"

"Something like that," I reply, pulling a small pistol from the holster on his belt.

"That's better, in a way. There's something big going on here, bigger than you could ever imagine. Now, if you found me down here, that means you have some intelligence, hmm? A smart girl like you could be rather useful in the days to come."

I turn him around and thrust my knee into his stomach, causing him to double over. "Flattery will get you nowhere asshole. I don't cut deals with people who think dogfights are…"

"Oh, you're that investigator woman." He coughs. "Private, I assume? You didn't flash a badge."

"That's right," I say, making a point of keeping my gun trained on him. "You'll be meeting the badge wielders soon enough, though."

"I don't think I will be." He smiles arrogantly.

I barely notice his hand swipe out in time to sidestep his attack. Turns out the thick buckle on his belt wasn't a poorly designed decorative lump of metal but a detachable switchblade. It also turns out that Malcolm Castleford doesn't have a clue how to use a knife. One swift kick sends the weapon flying, and within seconds I have him back up on his feet, pressed up against the wall with my arm across his throat. "You want to try that again?"

"Tam, wasn't it?" he mutters. "I meant what I said. There are changes coming, and there's no reason you can't be on board for them."

"Allen Fuerza has hired me to make sure you make it to the police station in one piece. That's one reason."

"Ah." Castleford swallows hard and I feel his Adam's apple bob against my forearm. "Tell me. Do you know who your client is? Or what he's trying to hide?"

"I'm not paid to worry about what he's trying to hide. Now, get moving."

I step back and bring my gun back up, but Castleford doesn't move.

"And why should I do that? There's no guarantee that Mr. Fuerza won't kill me the moment I step outside."

"With that new Paloma of his, if he'd wanted you dead, you would be already."

"*New Paloma*... A tall man, correct? Dark skin, shaven head, a scar under his left eye?"

"That's him."

"I thought so. In that case, I'm *surprised* I'm not dead already. Still, it does prove that I was right." He smiles and steps quickly to a small table, ignoring the gun I'm still training on him. He starts rummaging through the papers resting on top and mumbles, "Now, where should I start?"

"You start by backing away from the table, Mr. Castleford. I would rather finish this job as per my client's instructions, but if you don't get moving, that may become an impossibility."

"Really?" He asks and lifts a copy of a hardback book up to look at. I note that it's another copy of *Four Steps to Power* by Casille di Franco. "And why's that?"

"The Dealers know about the dogfight. They know you used *their* tunnels to get people there, and they know you're getting ready to make some big reveal. They've already contacted the Sweepers."

Castleford freezes in his paper-rummaging and glances over his shoulder. "How did they find out? That isn't the sort of move Fuerza would make."

"*I* told them."

Castleford nervously scrunches the piece of paper in his hand. After a moment, he takes a deep breath and starts talking quietly to himself. "The Sweepers won't listen to reason, they're just paid grunts. Very talented grunts, but very single-minded... The Dealers, though, they're business people, I could... No, I'd rather not deal with that step just yet. One thing at a time..."

The stern voice isn't working. Time to revert to the physical approach. That at least got a reaction out of him.

I storm across the room and shove the papers off the table, then grab Castleford's shirt and spin him harshly around. Before he can even stop stumbling, I bring the barrel of the Glock back up to the back of his head and push, just hard enough to make him move towards the exit. "Keep your hands where I can see them and lead the way out," I tell him, keeping my voice in a low growl.

"Police or Dealers," Castleford sighs, raising his arms. "I suppose that the end result is the same either way. I still hold the cards after all."

"Move."

Castleford nods and starts walking. "You said that Mr. Fuerza wants me delivered to the police station. Do you happen to know why he wants me alive?"

We turn another corner and start heading away from the way I came in. I wouldn't normally answer too many questions from a target, but the answer for this has the added sting of pointing out that this idiot's lower than the least successful gangster in New Hopeland. "He wants you to remember your place."

"Ah." Castleford laughs. "So, he still thinks I could be useful to him. You know, it's a fair way to the exit. Perhaps you would permit me to put my hands down?"

"Do anything stupid and I shoot you in the arm."

Castleford nods and drops his arms casually to his side, letting them fall into a gentle sway with his steps. "You said you aren't interested in what Mr. Fuerza is hiding, but believe me, Detective, it really is quite fascinating. How about I tell you a little about what I dug up? You know, to pass the time?"

"Do you *want* to draw the Sweepers to us?"

"You know how they work, I'm sure. If they're in the area, they'll find us whether I'm talking or not."

He has a point. Thinking about it, I'm surprised they haven't appeared yet. Thankful, but surprised. Maybe Sunglasses came through. And in fairness, I do want to know what I'm being used to protect. This could be my only chance to go yeti hunting. But it's one of those situations that comes with a "don't push your luck" tag.

"Like that ever stopped me," I grumble to myself, then add, louder, "Fine. Talk."

"I think you'll appreciate this on a professional level. Finding out what I did took some sleuthing, and some damn good sleuthing, if I do say so myself. In fact, yes, let's make a game of this. You'll enjoy that. Among those papers you scattered were some account summaries, that's where it all starts. You see, I do the accounting for a number of Fuerza's business interests, both legal and otherwise. Can you guess what the one constant that all his businesses have as an ongoing expenditure is?"

"Not a clue."

"Monthly fees to some larger, unrelated companies. The first working day of each month, five percent of his earnings go to Bockenheim Electrical Services, Grant and Thatcher Legal Group, Sand and Salt, and Kendle and

Sons Warehouses. What do you notice about those names? I'll give you a clue. There are four of them, and you could say they control part of Mr. Fuerza's money. His livelihood if you will. Understanding this is the *initial* step to understanding the bigger picture."

I frown, running the names through my head again. Bockenheim Electrical Services, Grant and Thatcher Legal Group, Sand and Salt, and Kendle and Sons Warehouse. He put an emphasis on the word initial. Initials? BES, GTLG, SS, KSW. Four of them, in control... Ah, it's only the first and last initial that matters. "Brett Stantz, Gory Gutierrez, Saul Solomon, and Kerry White. The Four Kings of Utah."

"Exactly."

"That's not a big deal. The Kings taking a cut from everyone below them is common knowledge."

"Yes, but when you're following the money to ensure that everything adds up, you start to spot other things. For example, the Kings have one accountant who has access to all their accounts, and his name comes up quite a bit as being related to some of the other businesses Mr. Fuerza is involved with. Now, the way it all works is that the money Fuerza makes is funnelled through multiple steps before he sees it in any tangible form. Aliases, false businesses, legitimate endeavours, they all intertwine in this web of asset movement. Without access to all of it, or all the important parts anyway, it's incredibly hard to trace. It minimises taxes and so on if you can keep some of it off the radar."

"Tax dodging is *not* worth setting up a dogfight for," I say through gritted teeth.

"Oh, I quite agree. Here's where things get interesting. You see, I keep my working papers immaculately neat. Separate columns for different things, standard widths to keep it all in line, and so on. You could say I'm somewhat of a column connoisseur. A columnnoisser if you will." When I don't laugh at his joke, Castleford lets out an embarrassed cough and continues, "It pays not to leave too many things to chance in my line of work, but sometimes, chance can lead you down such wonderful paths.

"There I was, laying out the latest combined figures in strict date order, and I noticed something amusing about the first initials of the various recipients of a number of deals that had crossed over in the timeline. When you looked at them in order, they spelled out a name: di Franco. Now, at first, I couldn't figure out where I knew the name from. It wasn't until I was visiting Mr. Fuerza's warehouse to check some figures that I realised where I'd seen it. He has a book he likes to read quite often, you see."

"*Four Steps to Power* by Casille di Franco. He had a copy of it with him when I spoke to him about the Tapping."

"Aha, so it was you who let him in on that. But how did…? Of course, the owner of one of the dogs must have hired you. I see, I see, that makes sense. But I digress. I mentioned the coincidence to Mr. Fuerza and, as you would expect, he had no sense of humour about it. In fact, he became quite cagey. I figured he was just having a bad day, of course, it often happens, but something about his reaction stuck with me. To this day, I don't know what it was, but my interest was piqued."

"So you started digging," I state.

"Of course! And the first place I looked was the book. It wasn't a title I was overly familiar with, you see, so I did some research. Do you happen to know what it's about, Detective?"

"Vaguely."

"Tell me what you remember. It's important. Be brief, but cover the main points."

"Fine," I sigh. "Four guys meet online to complain about the current batch of politicians. They decide to band together to rig the next presidential election and, by focusing on one quarter of the country each, they manage to get a good idea of what the voters are likely to band together over. Realising they can't *all* run for President, they hire a proxy to run in their place and act on their instructions. Their thinking was that, if no one knew *they* were in control, then people would be more willing to talk freely with them, and they could use that to ensure continued support *if* the plan worked. Despite the differing societal views of their respective quarters, their campaign is cohesive enough to gain their proxy a comfortable win. Time goes on and both the proxy and the invisible joint Presidents manage to enact some positive changes, all bound together by some ironclad paperwork.

"Things start to go wrong when the IRS spots that some of the President's charitable donations appear to be going to four certain individuals at opposite corners of the USA, and said foursome go into panic mode. They decide to have the President carry out a series of diversionary tactics to draw the public's attention but, when they order an air strike on a third world country, accompanied by a swathe of false evidence of wrongdoings for the President to use as a justification, the proxy decides he's had enough. He comes clean and reveals all his secrets, gets removed from power, and all five are placed on trial. The book ends with each of the five lamenting what could have been and questioning whether the espionage was even necessary in the first place. Sound about right?"

"Spot on. Four people controlling one to hide their power. Take away the hiding part, and it's a sentiment that rings true for every member of the Utah Underworld, I'm sure. That probably explains why the book is so popular among the higher earners of the Underground."

Now, that I didn't know. It would make sense, though. It doesn't really strike me as Charlie's sort of book either, so she was probably wanting to see if I'd see the parallel.

"I did some research into the author," Castleford continues, "just to see if he had any other such works, but he was the once-and-done type. The book was slated by the general public and the young author took it all to heart, disappearing from public view shortly after."

"I'm getting bored, Castleford. Right now, it still sounds like tax dodging is the only thing you've got on Fuerza."

"And there was me thinking you'd appreciate the journey. Fine, fine. It took me a few days to notice, but not all of the aliases whose initials were involved in the di Franco anagram belonged to Mr. Fuerza. Two of them were regular, known aliases for Saul Solomon and Brett Stantz respectively. So, I ran through the figures again and found that if you took the initials from role-appropriate comparative aliases for Gory Gutierrez and Kerry White, then threw in a few more of Mr. Fuerza's less utilised identities, and two other aliases linked to all four Kings, you got..." Castleford glances back at me.

"Casille."

"Exactly. Had all the aliases belonged to Mr. Fuerza, I would have just assumed it was an intentional tribute. Or even an obsession. Given the links to the Kings, though..."

I frown. *The cover of the book in Fuerza's place was printed backwards. That has to be significant.* My breath catches, and I suddenly realise both where Castleford's logic is heading, and what his likely end game is. "If you're saying what I think you are, then...you're trying to take over the Underground..."

Castleford smiles but doesn't answer. He nods his head towards a large metal pipe and adds, "There's the exit."

We have to squat to get through. I can't say I'm a fan of the thick slimy stuff that's spread over the bottom part of the tube, but at least I'm nearly done with this.

Or not.

Chapter Nine

THE MOMENT WE make it out into the sun, it becomes very apparent that the Dealers decided to just post Sweepers at the tunnel exits. In this case, we're faced with three armed men who look like they've just stepped out of a tour with the military. One of them lifts his arm to his face and says, "Found them, tunnel two-B."

"Watch communicator, eh? Fancy."

The Sweeper nods to me and says, "Our orders are to take Mr. Castleford to speak with the Elites. *You* are free to go unless you try to interfere."

Well, that's just great. I should probably thank Charlie for this, and genuinely. If they'd been out for my blood too, it would have been easier, because I'd have no choice but to stand against them.

"It's fine," Castleford says. "If they're taking me to talk to the Elites, I can cut a deal. They'll want in on this, I'm certain. You should come too, Detective. So you can see how the story ends."

I glare at Castleford, doing my best to cut through his stupidity. "Think about what they know already. You're planning to publicly reveal a big secret about *your employer*, Allen Fuerza."

"He's only one of my employers, but yes."

"That's your problem."

Castleford screws his face up in confusion, clearly trying to think through what I could mean.

"I dated an Elite," I state flatly. "What you're planning to reveal doesn't matter, because the Dealers are your employers too. If you can sell out one employer, you can sell out another. The best you can hope for now is that they'll take what information you have and use it themselves after you're buried."

Castleford pales at that and starts glancing around, clearly considering making a run for it. One of the Sweepers raises his rifle and grunts, "I wouldn't."

The guy with the communicator sighs and says, "I hate to hurry you, but the offer of leaving unharmed is time limited."

I doubt that Sunglasses is gonna be happy if I just hand Castleford over. But these guys aren't gonna be happy if I try to stop them either. Think, Cassie.

While I'm busy trying to figure what exactly my options are, the Sweeper closest to the sewer tunnel entrance turns to peer around the side of the pipe and a loud *crack* breaks the silence. Devin Carmichael darts out from beside the pipe before the first Sweeper has finished falling and throws a knife into the communicator guy's hand, causing him to drop his rifle. The Sweeper closest to Castleford is too slow to readjust his aim and soon finds himself flipped over Devin's shoulder. Devin follows up by smacking the guy in the face with his own rifle, all without letting go of his arm. He turns just as the communicator guy steps in, ducks under a punch, then fires off two of his own, rocking the guy's head to the side, and sending him spinning to the ground.

With all three Sweepers unconscious, Devin adjusts his cowboy hat and smiles at me. "Ya know, darlin', this wasn't exactly what I had in mind when I said to avoid any avalanches."

I roll my eyes but return his smile. "What are you doing here, Devin?"

"Getting you two outta here. C'mon," he replies and starts jogging back around the side of the tunnel. I nod after him and Castleford follows silently, his face still pale. I guess that's what happens when you realise you've underestimated the consequences of your actions.

Devin leads us to his car. It's a Dodge Challenger SRT Hellcat in a metallic red, refurbished with all the expected mod cons. How he's managed to keep it so pristine out here, I'll never know. He sniffs quietly and pushes the rim of his hat back, then turns his head towards the exit. I follow his line of sight and see that we're in one of the older industrial sites.

"We're gonna have company on the way to the station," he says. "It's a shame you don't drive, Caz. How's your shooting on the move?"

"I can drive," Castleford offers, but shuts up when Devin gives him a pitying look.

"Key word is *don't*," I sigh. "I *can* drive, I just don't have a steady enough income to keep up with insurance payments and general upkeep."

"How long's it been since you were behind a wheel?"

I shrug. "A little over a year. My driving will still be better than my shooting, though."

"That'll have ta do," he says and tosses me the keys. He grabs Castleford and chucks him on the back seat, then hops in beside him and starts checking over a small artillery stash of high powered guns he's got stored in the back of the front passenger seat. I jump into the driver's seat and, after a small-but-embarrassing amount of stalling, we pull out onto the main road. "Keep slow for now," Devin advises. "No need to draw attention to ourselves just yet."

"I've gotta say, I'm glad Sunglasses sent *you* rather than one of Fuerza's normal goons."

"Sunglasses?" Devin laughs. "Well, I suppose he doesn't ever take the things off. What do ya call me? Cowboy Hat?"

"Oh, I've got a ton of pleasant names, just for you."

Devin laughs again and cocks another gun. "You're gonna want to speed up now, Caz. That black van we passed back there is about to start following us."

"Great," I mumble and pull out beside the car in front, hitting the gas as I do, so that we can overtake.

The sound of gunfire rings out behind us, and I can see the bullets ricocheting off the back window in the rearview mirror. I fight not to panic and swerve around another car while Devin pops up out of the sunroof, fires off a few shots, and drops back down again. "This'd be so much easier if I was trying to kill them," he grumbles.

"Any reason you aren't?"

"I'm hopin' that's gonna be obvious before death becomes a necessity," he replies and pops up for another round.

I swing us around a corner and immediately start heading for another, speeding across oncoming traffic like oh so many idiots I've yelled at before me. As I near the end of the street, another van skids out across the path and someone leans out the window, pointing a handgun right at me. They squeeze the trigger and fire off three quick shots. Devin's windscreen holds better than my nerve, and I hit panic mode, slamming on the brakes and sending the car into a spin. We collide with the second van, jolting the shooter back, and that buys me enough time to find the accelerator again. I slam my foot down, and we rocket forward, barely managing to swerve past the first van as it rounds the corner.

"Keep calm, Caz," Devin says. "You've had a gun in your face before."

"Yeah, but I've also been in a position to fight back. That's not so easy with your hands on a steering wheel."

We tear through the street the wrong way, sending several other cars screeching onto the sidewalk as they lose our accidental game of chicken. Eventually, I hit another turning and manage to get us back on track, but by then, both vans are once again on our tail and have spread themselves across both sides of the road. The front passenger in one fires off a few rounds and Devin tries to pop up to return fire, but the second van's passenger immediately unleashes off a few rounds of his own. "Damn," Devin growls. "They're working in relay."

Devin grabs a small handgun and reaches the barrel up through the sunroof. He turns his head back towards the rear window and squeezes the trigger, trying to get a decent aim. The first clip empties with no damage done, and he quickly switches it out and goes straight back to firing. A stray shot manages to catch one of the van's wing mirror's just as the front passenger leans out, and the guy yanks his body back into the vehicle.

We're still too far from the station. And what happens when we get there? Sweepers won't worry about shooting someone right in front of the cops if they have to. I slam my hand onto the horn, sending a pedestrian scurrying for the safety of the footpath, then glance at the rearview mirror again. It's beginning to look like we're pulling away from them. *No, wait. They're stopping. Why are they stopping?*

Devin stares out the back window and says, "If they ain't back by the time we pass the car dealership two blocks on, pull over."

I nod and do as he says, eventually bringing us to a stop in the car park behind said dealership. "What's going on?"

"Sunglasses, as you so eloquently called him, came through. They're off our backs."

"Why?" Castleford asks.

"Because you've now got yourself a choice. See, you're gonna be delivered to the police, just like Caz here planned. When you get there, you're gonna be interviewed by Donal O'Brien. You know *that* name, right?"

Castleford nods and Devin turns to me. "Caz, I gotta ask. Did he tell you what he dug up on the esteemed Mr. Fuerza?"

"Not entirely. I think I can piece the rest together, though."

"Well, shit." Devin pauses. I catch a nervous twitch on his lips as he says, "Sum up what you think you know, but be careful with your wording. You never know who's listening."

I turn to Castleford and narrow my eyes. "I think I know who Allen Fuerza really is."

Devin sighs. "You know that list I said you're on?" I nod, and he pats my back. "Be thankful for that. When this whole hoo-ha is over, I recommend you call me. If certain questions are asked, I ain't gonna be able to cover for you, but I may be able to do something else."

That means I'm right. Great.

I shoot Castleford a dark look, designed to demonstrate that I blame him entirely for the shit storm I'm gonna be stepping into. In case that wasn't clear enough, I snap one of my favourite insults at him for good measure. "*Puk gaai.*"

Devin, now confident that I'm fully aware of my situation, strolls casually over to Castleford and fires off a quick jab at his face. The accountant cowers back from him, and he smiles. "That one weren't for Caz. If she wants to hit you, she can, and it'll likely be harder than that. That was for the dogfight. Now, when we get to the police station, you're gonna behave yourself, right?"

Castleford nods in response, and Devin raises his hand again, causing the accountant to whimper. Rather than hit him again, Devin simply gives his thinning grey hair a patronising, if overly rough, ruffling. "Donal's gonna make sure you don't spill anything about *any* of your employers to anyone you shouldn't. If you do, he ain't gonna remember any of it, and when they find you the next mornin', everyone's gonna think you hung yourself. So, these are your options. One, you can keep quiet, bar admitting your guilt. You'll be sentenced, you'll go to prison, and you'll be given a task to do. Two, you talk, and you die."

I guess Castleford's bravado when I found him was because he thought he'd be able to cut a deal with just about anyone. Once he realised he was out of options, reality set in quickly, and now he has no fight left. "I'll do what Mr. Fuerza asks," he says.

I switch out and let Devin take the wheel for the remainder of the journey, and by *let,* I mean that I comply with his request to switch places so he can stop me wrecking his pride and joy. Once we get moving, I dial Lieutenant Hanson.

"Cassie?" she answers. "Shouldn't you be hunting for our devious little accountant?"

"Devious," I repeat with a smile. "I'm guessing you found the evidence you were looking for, then?"

"You *could* say that. That does mean your time's nearly up, though."

"I guess so. Ask me how the search is going."

"Oh boy," she chuckles. "Hey, Cassie, how's the search going?"

"I've got him here with me right now, and I'll be delivering him to the station within the next thirty minutes or so, depending on traffic."

"Well, thank you for saving me some time on the paperwork. You better stick around when you get there. We'll need to do the usual."

"Another interview? And here's me without my makeup," I reply, my voice dripping with mock upset.

Hanson laughs. "I'll see ya there," she says and hangs up.

"So, who's Donal O'Brien?" I ask.

Castleford remains silent, and I catch Devin checking on him in the rearview mirror. Devin lets the silence hang for a moment then responds, "He's one of the officers with ties to the Kings. If someone's deemed a danger to the running of the New Hopeland Underworld, then he gets to do the questioning. There are men and women like Donal O'Brien in every single one of Utah's police departments. *Sunglasses* contacting the Elites probably gave them a shock, but Donal being involved would have been key to getting the Sweepers to back off. It shows that the Kings have stepped in to restore the peace."

"The ones like Donal. Do *they* know?"

"What you figured out?" I nod, and Devin continues, "Most won't. Donal does, though."

"Given how scary he is, I'm guessing that Sunglasses is part of the King's Guard, isn't he?"

"Yup. Technically, all of those who know the truth are. Or they are if they were told rather than finding out themselves."

"Huh. And what are the ones that figured it all out by themselves?"

"Dead, mostly."

And that's enough to silence me for a while. It's funny, really. I didn't do the digging myself this time, I let someone else do it and kinda piggy-backed their knowledge instead, but the result was the same. I still let it go too far for me to back out.

BY THE TIME I make it back to my block, to say I'm tired would be an understatement. The police interviews took so long that they'd already dealt with Castleford and chucked him in a cell before I came close to getting out of there. I know it was all because he'd figured out how deep a hole he'd dug for himself and so gone along without the usual dancing around questions that a lot of the newly arrested give. It still annoys me that I had to spend longer explaining myself than the actual criminal did. Trying to convince the interviewing officers that they didn't need me to name certain people was frustratingly difficult too, thanks entirely to Lieutenant Hanson offloading some city rookies on me. Did seeing her sitting there laughing her ass off at the situation help at all? No, it did not.

To her credit, Hanson did eventually step in and explain a few things before I could get worked up to the level of violence, but by then, Fuerza and Sunglasses had turned up to give their own statements and visit Castleford. That I had to stop and let them know what I had and hadn't spilled rather than just calling them on my way home meant even more delays. Yeah, they did ask if Castleford had told me what he knew. I told them the same thing I told Devin. Fuerza insisted on making an appointment to see me tomorrow afternoon at his warehouse so we could *discuss* things.

With all that weighing on me, you can imagine how tired I am now that I've finally washed and slipped into some loose-fitting sleep clothes.

I glance at the clock and note it's not quite 10:00 p.m. yet. Almost instinctually, I grab my phone from the table, call up Lori's number, and slide my thumb across the screen to hit dial...but I stop. *Something's wrong here. I'm nervous, but not normal nervous. This isn't me worrying about saying something stupid, it's something else. But what?*

I move my thumb away from the little green dial logo and Devin's words come back to me.

"You know that list I said you're on? Be thankful for that. When this whole hoo-ha is over, I recommend you call me. If certain questions are asked, I ain't gonna be able to cover for you, but I may be able to do something else."

"What am I trying to say to her? That the last two months have been really great, and I want her to know how much I've enjoyed being around her? Why now? What am I doing?" I lean back on the couch and stare up at the ceiling light, letting the truth of it all settle in. "I'm gearing up to say goodbye."

"Caw?" Bert asks, and I let my eyes drift down far enough to see that he's taken up residence opposite me. He must have picked up on my mood.

"I'm just tired," I reply. "Nothing to worry about."

Bert lets out a mechanical chirp, and hunkers down into a more relaxed pose.

I wasn't lying. Today has been too overwhelming to think things through properly, which is why I'm feeling like I've lost already. That I thought it was important to say goodbye to Lori is something I can hold on to, because it will serve as a reminder of what I want to avoid. I won't call her until I've fixed this. The temptation to tie up loose ends is there, and if I do that, then I'll be walking into tomorrow having already decided I'm not getting out of this one alive. All that does is potentially create a self-fulfilling prophecy scenario for myself. I *will* call her, though. I *will* tell her how crap today's been, and I *will* use some of the money Fuerza owes me to treat her because the last two months really have been great. *That's* my aim. I don't want a quick exit or to go down in a blaze of glory, I want more time. More time with *her.*

I glance at Bert again and say, "Hey, Bert. Make sure you keep your power levels up. I need you on patrol tonight, just in case, but I'm gonna need you to do something specific for me tomorrow."

"Caw."

THE MORNING COMES quickly, and I end up spending longer in the shower than I would normally. It's not that I'm worried so much about appearances today, it's more that I want to make sure I'm fully awake. The first thing I do once I'm ready is call Devin.

"Morning," he answers. "I was getting worried when you didn't call me after you left the station."

"Yeah? You know what's going on then?"

"Not exactly. I figured you'd come clean, so when I didn't hear from ya... Well, you know what you're dealing with now. If you're calling now, though, then that means Fuerza's called a meeting, ain't he?"

I sigh. "I'm only gonna get one shot at this, aren't I?"

"That's the way it normally goes."

"In that case, I need to hire you for a job."

Devin goes quiet for a moment. "This is only gonna go one way or the other, Caz, and a lot of that is gonna come down to *you* and whether you're looking at this the right way." He pauses again, then says, "I'll tell ya what. Name the job. If it's the right one, I'll do it for free. If it's the wrong one, you're on your own."

"That clean-cut, eh?"

"Like I said, it goes one way or the other. There ain't a third outcome here."

"When I was getting ready to call you, I considered hiring you to make sure Fuerza doesn't kill me."

"But…" Devin prompts, and I can hear the smile in his voice.

"But there's a reason that neither Allen Fuerza nor any of the Four Kings have ever been arrested." I swallow and play my one card. "Devin Carmichael. I want to hire you to make sure that, for the duration of the meeting, *no one in Fuerza's employ* kills me."

Devin laughs, and says, "I'll pick you up in twenty minutes."

WE ARRIVE AT the warehouse to find Sunglasses waiting to greet us. I'd done Fuerza the favour of letting him know I'd hired Devin to accompany me, not because I'm kind, but because I didn't want to throw any unexpected surprises at him. Shock is a risky element to bring into *any* situation, but it's one that works to your advantage in a lot of circumstances. This is *not* a scenario where causing panic is going to help me. Besides, I doubt it changes Fuerza's plans for the day.

"The warehouse is empty, bar myself and Mr. Fuerza," Sunglasses states as he guides us inside.

"I figured it would be," I reply.

"Good," he says. "I am glad that you clearly understand the situation. For what it's worth, you are yet to disappoint me, Miss Tam."

"Good to know."

Sunglasses leads us up a set of stairs and into a room I not only didn't know existed but that I doubt anyone would *expect* to find in the building. It's a circular space, well lit, and immaculately carpeted in a wine-red colour that compliments the fancy green walls. Less surprising than the room, at least to me, is the clear difference in demeanour of its only other occupant compared to the last time I saw him. Allen Fuerza is still confident, but the feel is more relaxed than his normal exaggeration of the trait. This isn't a low-end, wannabe crime lord. This is someone who *knows* he will decide the outcome today.

"Miss Tam." He gives a slow nod. When I don't reply, he says, "I was glad to hear that you still intended to join us today. That you brought Mr. Carmichael with you means you understand the gravity of the situation. It also means you intend to walk away from here alive and well, one way or another, correct?"

"I do."

Fuerza nods to Sunglasses, who walks across the room and takes up residence to his left. "No sign of the Familiar?"

"He's not here," I answer for Sunglasses. "I sent him over to watch Lori Redwood."

"Redwood... The Tech Shifter girl?" I nod and Fuerza continues, "Then you two must be... You think that I would target your girlfriend?" he asks, a hint of disappointment in his voice.

I shake my head. "Not really, no. But I'd rather play things safe. Plus, he has a habit of acting on his own authority. Right now, Bert busting in and going nuts won't help either of us. Having a set task reduces the risk of that."

"That is appreciated, Miss Tam. Tell me, did you spend the hours I gave you making sure your affairs are in order?"

"Nope."

Fuerza chuckles and shakes his head. "You *are* confident, aren't you?"

"If I wasn't, it would have been pretty stupid of me to turn up at all, wouldn't it?"

"Often times," Sunglasses interjects, "those who find themselves in your situation simply accept their fate."

"Yeah, well, I never did like other people deciding my fate for me."

"In that case," Fuerza replies, "how about we let you get on with deciding *your own* fate, hmm? I understand Mr. Castleford told you some of his methods, but not the end result of his research. How about you tell me what you believe the result is? You have my word that I will confirm if you are correct. Under the circumstances, I think it would be fair if I were to offer a correction if you are wrong too, don't you?"

I take a deep breath and start to potentially throw my life away. "It all comes back to the book, *Four Steps to Power* by Casille di Franco. Honestly, having the name of the author spelled out by the initials of your aliases was pretty stupid. I know the possibility of all the aliases lining up in the right order was ridiculously low, but anyone with access to the data had the potential to spot the pattern if even only a few of the letters lined up."

Sunglasses smirks and says, "Insults?"

"*I* got myself into this mess, and *I'm* gonna get myself out of it. That means *all* of me, personality and all."

"Please, continue," Fuerza says, nonchalantly waving me on.

"It *could* have just been that you're a really big fan of the book. That's what Castleford thought initially. I would have thought the same thing if I'm being honest. Even using the King's aliases as part of an anagram could have been passed off as a crude joke, maybe even a form of hero worship aimed at those at the top of your profession. Your reaction, though, that tipped Castleford off. That he took this as far as he did means he's either an idiot, or he found something else. *This—*" I wave my hand at the room "—tells me the latter applies. My guess is he followed the money deep enough into the mud to see what was lurking underneath. You had access to all the accounts involved. Once he figured that out, it wouldn't have been hard to come up with a closer link between you and the Four Kings than the expected one."

"Good. And what is the link, do you think?" Fuerza asks, flashing me a dangerous smile.

"Castleford sent you the copy of the book you had with you when we met during my previous case. The title was printed backwards. He was hinting that the book had the right idea but had it the wrong way around. This wasn't four people controlling one, it was one controlling four. That was my first thought, anyway. The thing is, you have access to all of those accounts. And no one ever sees the Kings in person. Allen Fuerza does not control the Four Kings of Utah, he *is* the Four Kings of Utah."

Sunglasses' arm rises quicker than I can track, aiming a gun at my head. At the same time, Devin's arm rises to meet the aim, his own gun pointed square at the only dangerous Paloma I've ever known. I choose to keep my eyes on Fuerza as far as possible. I trust Devin to keep me safe. Plus, even if not physically, it's Fuerza who will pull the trigger.

"Did you figure out the connection between myself and Casille di Franco too?"

"No."

"Then I will tell you that one as a gesture of goodwill. Casille di Franco was my birth name. If I were to tell you that my father was a successful, if unremarkable, member of the criminal underworld and that I had formulated certain plans prior to writing the book, what would you think?"

My lips twitch. "I'd say that...the book and the aliases were part of something intentional. You wanted to leave a trail people could follow, but only if they were on the inside. To search for potential allies?"

"If that were true, would you still think that the aliases spelling out the name was stupid?"

"Yup. To me, that's far too risky. I'd have stuck to hand-picking people."

"I do, mostly. Yes, I have found one or two allies through this method, but the primary purpose is to root out those who are potentially dangerous to my position. The curious ones, the ambitious ones. The ones who can neither give nor receive trust. If they can be cowed as Mr. Castleford has, all the better. If not, they disappear. Which brings me to today's business. Would you be willing to *beg* for your life, Miss Tam?"

"No."

"Good. If you had said yes, it would mean you would be likely to tell my secrets if given the right stimulus. In that case, explain to me why I shouldn't have you killed right now?"

"Ya can try," Devin chuckles, and Sunglasses responds to him with a confident nod.

I knew it would come down to this question, and I know what I want to say. I swallow hard and muster as much conviction as I can. "New Hopeland *works*."

Fuerza waits patiently for me to continue and, when it becomes clear I'm not going to, he bursts out laughing. "That's it? Your entire argument is just three words? Do you think yourself so integral to the city that it couldn't possibly continue without you?"

I shake my head. "New Hopeland will continue to work, with or without me. The system ensures that, even if most people never know the system even exists, much less what it is. Make no mistake. We are not, nor will we ever be, on the same page with this. But the fact is, I don't want to see this city, *my* city, fall into the shadows."

"So. You stand in protest of the Four Kings, but you have no intention of moving against them. And you take this position because you accept New Hopeland for what it is, warts and all," Fuerza summarises. He sighs deeply and adds, "Good enough."

And with that, both Sunglasses and Devin lower their guns.

"You are smarter than many I have had eliminated," Fuerza says. "And you are further from loyal to me than I would normally tolerate. But you care about New Hopeland itself, and you understand the balance in play better than most. You may leave, Detective. But know that we will be watching. The slightest hint at a betrayal of my kindness will be all it takes."

I nod, turn, and walk away from the scariest man in New Hopeland, with Devin at my back. We get as far as the door before Fuerza adds, "Oh, and feel free to pass your payment details over through whatever means you deem most appropriate. I believe I owe you a sum of money."

I wave without turning around, and we keep walking. Once we're out of the building and sitting comfortably in his car, Devin turns to me and comments, "That was risky, darlin'."

"I know."

"The thing is, Caz, the people in this city *need* someone to control them. For most of the Underground, it's gotta be the Four Kings, 'cause they symbolise an absolute and terrifying power. Without Allen Fuerza, the low-end, idiotic, laughing stock of criminal society, the Kings wouldn't have the knowledge to rule as effectively as they do. The moment the Kings aren't there to keep the scum in line, we're all going to Hell in a handbasket."

"I know."

"And you know there's more to why Fuerza is doing this, don't you?"

"Yup."

"Then let me ask you something. I know full well that you meant every word you said in there, and so does Fuerza, or he wouldn't have let you leave. If you aren't on *his* side, but you're not going against him, where *do* your loyalties lie?"

I smile. "I stand with the people of New Hopeland. For better or for worse."

Devin lets out a whispered chuckle and repeats Fuerza's words. "Good enough, Caz. Good enough. So, where to now? Back to your office?"

"Nah. I'm gonna head over to my girlfriend's and spend some time relaxing. She got me started down this path to begin with, so if nothing else, she can make me a coffee. I think I need it at this point."

Devin nods and starts up the Hellcat. "I'll drop you off."

Tech Shift Gear Welcome Pack

Thank you for considering Shift Source Ltd for your roleplay needs. As the only producers of the patented Tech Shift Gear system, we take our customers' safety very seriously. Due to the nature of the system, the safety processes begin the moment you make us aware of your interest in purchasing one of our products. This welcome pack is designed to help you make an informed decision in relation to your potential purchase.

If after reading this pack, you are still interested in acquiring Tech Shift Gear of your own, you will first be put forward to undergo a full psychological evaluation. This is a legal requirement before we can implement the design and manufacturing process. Though simply a formality in the majority of cases, past misuse of the system by a small percentage of users has shown that not only do some individuals wish to use TS Gear for unlawful purposes but the plug insertion operation can potentially cause some emotional trauma for users. The evaluation allows us to weed out those with ill intent, and also offer impartial advice to those at a high risk of damage as a result of using the system.

Please note: No further information will be given regarding the psychological assessment in this pack, as to do so would allow those who seek to misuse the system to prepare strategies to falsely pass the evaluation.

Most importantly, please remember that Tech Shifting is supposed to be fun. This pack has been produced because we at Shift Source Ltd simply wish to ensure that the Tech Shift Gear system is the right choice...for you.

Thank you for your consideration.

Mr. D Hollister,
CEO, Shift Source Ltd

We shall now discuss individual sections of the TS Gear, running in the order that you would put each piece on when suiting up.

THE SPINE AND HEAD

We will begin by discussing the most invasive part of the process: the spine and head; both yours and your future suit's.

It is well known that to operate TS Gear, you will be required to undergo a medical procedure that will see rubber-tipped plugs inserted in your spine and head. The press has often cited this process as involving nano-technology that allows you to control your suit by sheer thought alone. Though such a step is not being ruled out once the necessary technological advancements have been made, this is not at present true. The actual process is far more mundane and shall be detailed below.

Prior to your operation, you would undergo a series of X-rays, each with you posing in a different position. This is so that several important measurements can be taken:

- The full length of your vertebral column

- The gap between each spinous process in each position

- The thickness of your skull

While the reasoning behind measuring the length of your vertebral column should be obvious, you may not be aware of why we measure gaps between spinous process (if you did not know, the spinous process is a protrusion on the outside of each disk in your vertebral column). This is because drilling holes into individual spinal discs would run a high risk of causing irreparable damage. Instead, the plugs are inserted at points between spinous processes. The X-rays taken mean that we can ascertain areas where there is a natural gap when you stand in different positions.

We are then also able to form an accurate replica of your vertebral column which will allow us to check the effects on your movement and flexibility that placing a plug where there is no gap would yield. These results would then be discussed with you prior to moving ahead. This process is also the reason that different people's TS Gear will have a different number of pins, and differing gaps between each pin.

But why is this operation necessary? Though TS Gear does not utilize (at time of writing, experimental) nano-technology, it does still utilise several other modern processes. The plug and pin system is designed to allow the TS Gear to be locked in place on your body. While the simple insertion of the pins into the plugs does serve this purpose, the weight of TS Gear means that this alone would not be sufficient to provide optimal safety and freedom of movement. In fact, early testing without this system in place showed that the weight of the suit often led to it slipping to the side when moving forcefully or at speed. As a result, we have built the suits with a small sensor fitted at the base of each pin. This sensor registers micro movements in your body. When it detects movement in an individual section, it activates a small magnet within the relevant pin that will ensure it remains in place.

Ensuring that the spine of the suit remains in place is integral to the smooth operation of the system, as this truly forms the central hub of the TS Gear. Let's look at the individual parts of the spine and what they do.

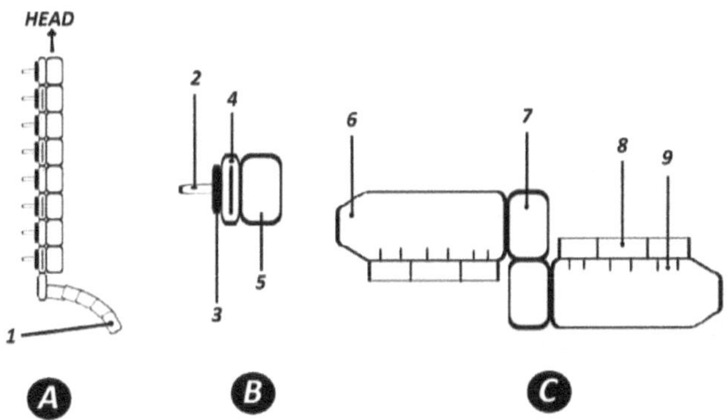

DIAGRAM A: THE SPINE (BELOW THE HEAD)

1. The tail. Situated at the base of the spine, this protrusion is built from multiple small sections and is controlled via a wireless touchpad within the hands/front legs of the suit.

DIAGRAM B: INDIVIDUAL PIN AND PLUG SECTION

2. The pin. This will vary in length from suit to suit, depending on the results of the initial X-rays.

3. The spinal plug. Situated at the base of each pin, the material naturally sticks to the plugs running along your spine. This section also contains the small motion sensor and magnetic control mentioned above.

NOTE: In sections where plugs cannot be placed, the TS Gear spine will feature several sections with no pin. The remainder of the section will be identical, bar the lack of a magnetic motion sensor. In these instances, an adhesive can be applied to the rubber plugs to combat the lack of an actual lock.

4. The strap lock. This is used to lock in the tips of the body straps.

5. The body strap. When not in use, each strap rolls itself into a neat tube at the top of the spine. When in use, they roll out and *snap* around the wearer's body, forming a skintight layer that locks into the strap lock on the opposite side to which they began unrolling.

DIAGRAM C: OPEN BODY STRAPS

6. The strap tip. This slight indent in the design allows the strip to slot into the strap lock on the relevant pin and plug section. This locks in a similar way to a magnet-enhanced seat belt in a motor vehicle.

7. Top down view of a strap lock.

8. Gap strips. These slide out from the side of the body strap and cover the small gaps between the individual body straps. Their bases maintain a natural level of viscosity that allows them to stick to the straps.

9. The strip casing. This houses the gap strips when not in use. Once a body strap has locked into a strap lock, they push the strips out. Each body strap has a gap strip on each side of its length.

NOTE: Body straps will vary in length, not only from person to person but from body section to body section.

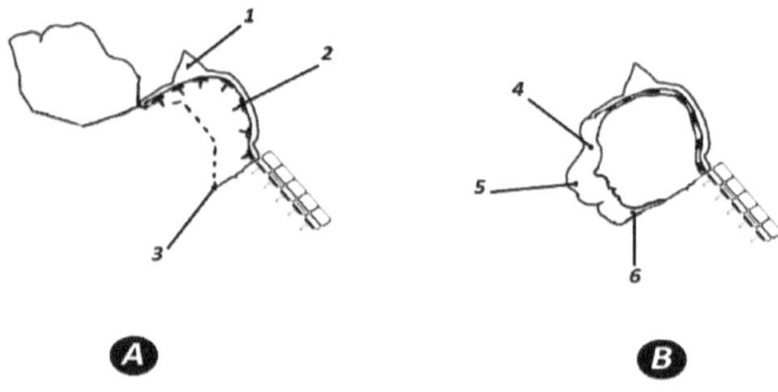

DIAGRAM A: THE HEAD (OPEN)

1. The ear. While ear positions on each head will vary (depending on your chosen species), the core system will remain the same. Each ear will be fitted with microphones that run down through the mask to a small speaker system placed next to your natural ears inside the mask. Volume can be adjusted with a small switch at the top of the speakers.

2. The pin. Naturally shorter than those on the spine, the purpose here is the same. They lock the head in place, and the plug contains a small magnet to assist in this.

3. The chin lock. This locks the front of the head in place when closed.

DIAGRAM B: THE HEAD (CLOSED)

4. The eyes. These will be placed in line with your own eyes. This may result in a slight distortion in the shape or size of your TS Gear head when compared with actual examples of your chosen species, but we will do our best to ensure authenticity without sacrificing sight. To keep this section in place, the inside of each eye hole is lined with small pins. It is not uncommon for this to lead to minor scarification for the wearer.

5. The nose. This will be aligned with your own nose as far as possible, but to ensure the ability to breathe, a lightweight pipe system will also be applied that can be inserted comfortably in your nostrils.

6. The chin. This sits snug to your own chin and is used to operate the mouth. In publicly available suits, the chin and jaw are enforced with a spring and magnet system that allows for a *snapping* effect on mouth movements.

NOTE: The head is thick but skintight. The pliable material used for TS Gear is designed to be able to move with your own face in order to allow not only free movement but physical expression.

THE BACK LEGS

Much like the spine and head, the back legs on TS Gear will not change, regardless of whether you are wearing an anthropomorphic hybrid or full animal suit. They are designed to mimic the actual legs of the animal you wish to roleplay as, but changes can certainly be made if you have a specific design in mind. For the purposes of this pack, we shall be looking at the digitigrade legs of a large feline.

First, it would be useful to understand the difference between the joints of a plantigrade human and a digitigrade feline. To illustrate this, we have produced a series of diagrams.

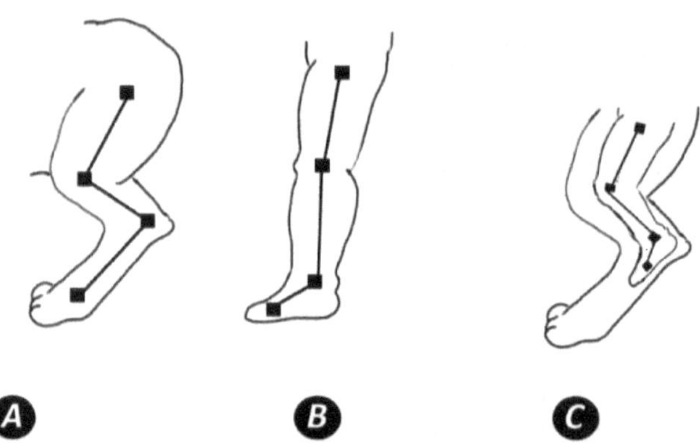

Diagram A above shows the digitigrade legs of a large feline. You will note that the *heel* of the animal is much higher up than that of a plantigrade human (Diagram B above), leading to an elongated foot. The way TS Gear works is to allow the human leg to slot inside the animal leg as per Diagram C above. Let's take a closer look at this process.

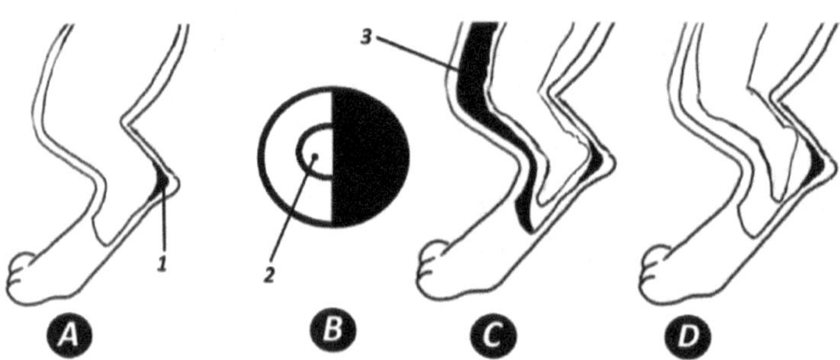

DIAGRAM A: EMPTY LEG

1. Heel pad. This is designed for comfort, but also includes one of the vital control systems of the leg.

DIAGRAM B: HEEL PAD

2. Pressure pad. When pressed by the wearer's heel, this activates the leg lock and hydraulic system.

DIAGRAM C: STANDING/WALKING LEG

3. Leg lock. When the wearer applies pressure to the pressure pad, this section inflates to ensure that the wearer's leg is held in place inside the TS Gear leg. When this section is inflated, a hydraulic lock is also engaged in the foot, preventing the TS Gear leg from collapsing. This is to stop the wearer from falling.

DIAGRAM D: NON-LOCKED LEG

When the wearer lifts their heel from the pressure pad, the leg lock will deflate, and the hydraulic lock in the foot will unlock. This allows the wearer to either dismount from the leg, or with some practice, lay down by shifting their leg position. Some wearers have also learned to manipulate this system to allow their TS Gear foot to sway as they walk, adding some personality to their character.

NOTE: The pressure pad is sensitive and only requires minimal pressure to activate.

THE FRONT LEGS

No diagrams have been included in relation to anthropomorphic hybrid suits for this section of the pack. The reason for this is that the front legs for this style of suit resemble human arms. With the exception of slightly elongated nails, the design is identical to that of the wearer and is built to fit exactly with no lengthening of the arms, much like a custom glove. They also require an inflatable no locking system. The only thing to note in this style of TS Gear is that each thumb contains a sensitive touchpad that registers micro movements. This is used to control the tail via a wireless system, with one hand responsible for the movement of the lower half of the tail and the other for the upper half. When it comes to full animal style TS Gear, the front legs are set up a little differently.

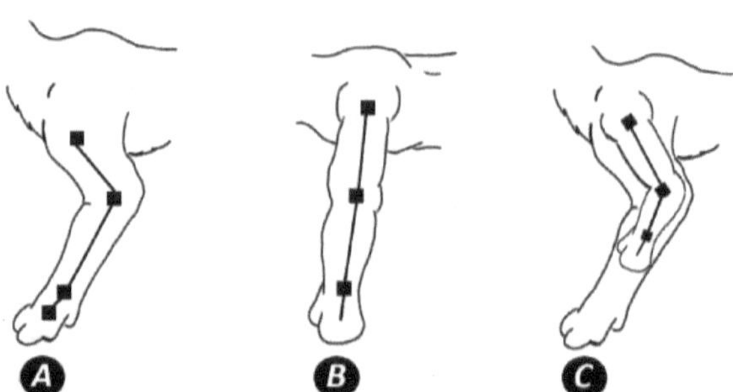

You will notice in Diagrams A and B above that the points of articulation in the front legs of a large feline and those of a human are broadly similar. Due to the way that the digitigrade back legs are formed, however, it is impossible to have the front legs of a full animal style suit matching the length of the wearer's arms without causing a disparity in size between the front and back legs. As such, the wearer's arms will be inserted as per Diagram C. Let's take a closer look at this.

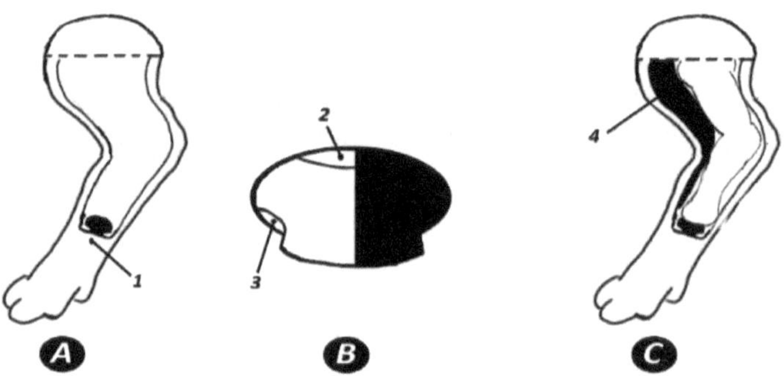

<u>DIAGRAM A: FRONT LEG EMPTY</u>

1. The pressure ball. This section controls both the arm lock and the tail movement.

<u>DIAGRAM B: THE PRESSURE BALL</u>

2. The primary pressure point. When gripped, the wearer's palm will apply pressure to this button, which will, in turn, inflate the arm lock.

3. The tail control. This thumb pad is responsible for wirelessly controlling tail movement. The movement will be split between both front legs with one being responsible for the lower half of the tail, and the other for the upper half.

<u>DIAGRAM C: FRONT LEG LOCKED</u>

4. The arm lock. When the arm lock is inflated, a hydraulic lock will also engage in the foot, ensuring that the wearer cannot fall. As with the back legs, simply removing pressure from the pad will deflate the arm lock and loosen the hydraulic lock, allowing the wearer to lie down. Again, some wearers have learned to manipulate this system to allow their TS Gear foot to sway as they walk, adding some personality to their character.

CONNECTING THE LEGS TO THE SUIT

With regards to both the back and front legs, each pair is connected by a series of strips, with the middle section made from a slightly hardened form of the body straps. This increased toughness allows the wearer to rest on the platform that the material creates when engaging or disengaging from the legs. It also gives the wearer something to rest on if fatigued. The only variance between the front and back legs in this respect is how they connect to the main suit.

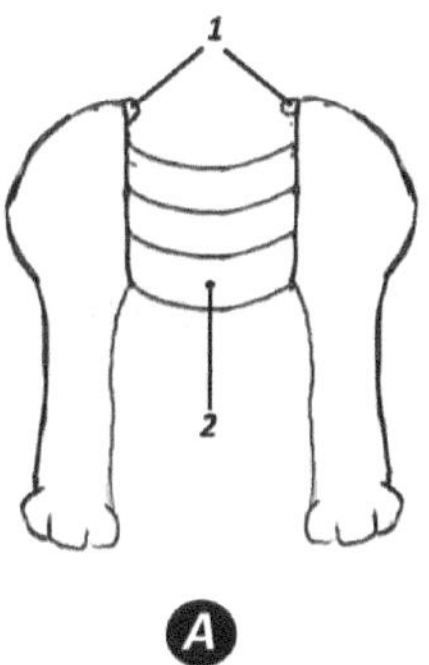

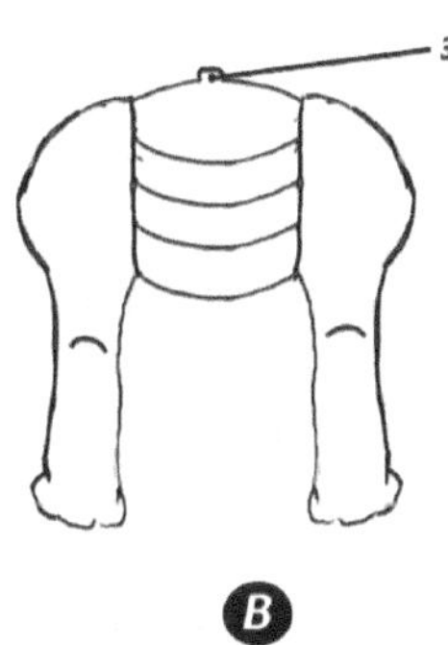

<u>DIAGRAM A: FRONT LEGS</u>

1. Shoulder couplings. These slot into the strap locks in the same way as the body straps.

2. Body sheet. These overlap in a similar way to the gap strips on the spine, and the uppermost layer slides in the same way. The base of the area is built to be stronger and less pliable, so as to act as support for the wearer when the suit is in use. The upper and rear end of the sheet meanwhile is far more pliable and more like the body straps attached to the spine.

<u>DIAGRAM B: BACK LEGS</u>

3. Rear coupling. The rear sheet is built the same as the body sheet on the front legs, with a stronger base but pliable upper and lower area. The point labelled sits at the uppermost end of the sheet and connects to a strap lock just below the tail in the same way as the body straps.

ADDITIONAL NOTES

You will note that the core human body is not identical to that of an animal. In this respect, the skintight nature of the TS Gear system means that simple workarounds can be put into place with ease. All TS Gear comes with the option of a free body altering undersuit. This will be primarily made of Lycra and will feature padding that will create the illusion of a more animalistic form beneath the engaged body straps.

It is also worth noting that both the pressure ball and heel pad require lubrication. The specialised formula the suits take can be ordered directly from Shift Source Ltd at minimal cost. While third-party versions are currently available, the use of these will void the warranty on the suit.

Should you choose to go ahead with your purchase, your TS Gear will be built entirely to your specifications, not only in terms of measurements but to a design of your choice. You will be given a full manual of operation and will also be invited to take part in a series of free lessons designed to help you learn how to operate your suit in a practical but safe environment.

Please, take your time in considering our product, and we hope to see you soon for your first full consultation.

About the Author

Matt Doyle lives in the South East of England and shares his home with a wide variety of people and animals, as well as a fine selection of teas. He has spent his life chasing dreams, a habit which has seen him gain success in a great number of fields. To date, this has included spending ten years as a professional wrestler, completing a range of cosplay projects, and publishing multiple works of fiction.

These days, Matt can be found working on far too many novels at once, blogging about anime, comics, and games, and plotting and planning what other things he'll be doing to take up what little free time he has.

Email: mattdoylemedia@hotmail.com

Facebook: www.fb.me/MattDoyleMedia

Twitter: @mattdoylemedia

Website: www.mattdoylemedia.com

Other books by this author

Addict

Coming Soon from Matt Doyle

LV48

The Cassie Tam Files, Book Three

Excerpt

"*Nei hou gaau siu.*"

When Lori smiles like that, her eyes take on a slight twinkle, making their pale blue tone feel warm and welcoming. That being the case, it takes me a moment to realize I didn't understand a word she just said. Am I so drunk already? "Uh, sorry. What?"

Lori giggles and repeats, "*Nei hou gaau siu.*" When I just stare blankly, she frowns and asks, "Is my pronunciation off? I was sure that was right."

"What were you trying to say?"

"I was trying to tell you that you're funny in Cantonese."

And at that, the laughter spills out of me, uncontrolled to the point I have to bury my face in the table to muffle the sound. If we'd been in our usual haunt, Northern Main Street's late-night cafe-cum-alternative hangout Tourniquet, I'd have just let loose uninhibited. The people there look like an odd bunch when you're viewing things from the outside, but if you spend enough time there, you soon realize they're all really nice people with tastes and hobbies that fall outside the mainstream. Seeing as we've opted for Cartwright's on Dunstone Avenue, I'm trying to hold back. Honestly, I am. I'm just not doing a good job of it.

The staff in Cartwright's are lovely, but the clientele is a little less raucous than those at Tourniquet, and so I'm already drawing some confused looks by the time I wipe the tears from my eyes. "I'm sorry," I say, "I'm sorry."

"I've never been much good at languages. Oh God," Lori sighs, and shoots me a now far more nervous smile. "Put me out of my misery. What did I just say?"

I shrug. "You probably just told me that I was funny in Cantonese."

Lori tilts her head and says, "Okay, now I'm confused."

"I don't speak Cantonese."

"Yes, you do."

"I really don't."

"You really do. I mean, you can't seriously be telling me you've been using *diu* in the Taiwanese sense?"

"No, no...," I reply, waving my hands in frantic motions. "Wait. What does it mean in Taiwan?"

"It was old slang for cool."

"Oh, right. No, I'm definitely using it the way you think."

"So you do speak Cantonese then."

"No, I swear in Cantonese. I couldn't hold a conversation in it. My dad had a thing about me swearing. He hated it, even when I was adult. It was the one thing that always made him roll his eyes at Mom. Anyway, he spoke Mandarin, English, and a little French, so my options for big kid words were kinda limited. I went to school with a guy named Tom Huang; he spoke Cantonese, so I got him to teach me the cool words. Dad probably got the gist of what I was saying, but I think he appreciated the ingenuity of it."

And now, Lori laughs, and buries her face in her hands. She shakes her head and says, "I am such an idiot."

"Nah, it's not like I've ever spoken Mandarin around you, so how would you know? Honestly, I know enough Mandarin to get by, but we always spoke English at home, so I just picked that up easier. Let's see, though...you would have meant *nǐ hěn gǎoxiào*. Or if you wanted to be really over the top with it, *nǐ jiǎng shénme dōu néng bǎ wǒ lè huài le*. That's 'everything that you say cracks me up.'"

Lori shakes her head. "I think I'll stick to English."

Also Available from NineStar Press

Connect with NineStar Press

Website: NineStarPress.com

Facebook: NineStarPress

Facebook Reader Group: NineStarNiche

Twitter: @ninestarpress

Tumblr: NineStarPress

www.ingramcontent.com/pod-product-compliance
Lightning Source LLC
Chambersburg PA
CBHW051706180726
48283CB00004B/1225